Toots
upside down again

Toots

upside down again

CAROL HUGHES

BLOOMSBURY

First published in Great Britain in 1998
Bloomsbury Publishing Plc, 38 Soho Square, London W1V 5DF

Copyright © Text Carol Hughes 1998

The moral right of the author has been asserted
A CIP catalogue record of this book is available from the
British Library

ISBN 0 7475 3436 5

Typeset by Dorchester Typesetting Group Ltd

Printed in Great Britain by Clays Ltd, St Ives plc

10 9 8 7 6 5 4 3

Cover design by Michelle Radford

For Mum and Ron

A Short Note on the
Upside Down-ness of It All

Every house has an Upside Down House, and every house with a garden has an Upside Down Garden, in much the same way as every school has an Upside Down School, and every playground has an Upside Down Playground.

'What is all this upside down-ness?' you may ask. It's just what it sounds like. The same place, but upside down. Only it isn't really the same place at all. You'd never know it was there unless you stood on your head, or hung backwards over a chair, because that's the only way you can see it.

When you first look at the world upside down it will probably look like nothing special at all, and you'll wonder what on earth I'm talking about, but if you're patient and quiet, you might see something you didn't expect to see sauntering across the ceiling or sitting on the bottom of a tree branch. And that's when you'll know you've seen some-one or something from the Upside Down World. Go on, try it now. Turn yourself the other way up and stare down at the ceiling or the sky and imagine what it would be like if the world was always that way up. What would happen if you fell into those clouds? You would probably fall for ever.

But, and here's the catch, if you've ever been to the Upside Down World, you won't remember because, although at the time everything seems very real, when you return to your own world the memory fades like a dream. That was how it was for Toots: she could barely remember Olive and the fairies and everything that had happened to her in the Upside Down House. That was until she met Olive again.

CHAPTER ONE

~ Spring ~

One bright, blustery April day just after Easter, Toots sat on the swing in her garden and shivered. Even though the sun was shining, a wintry wind rattled through the fence. It screamed across the lawn and shook the bare branches of the horse chestnut tree and sometimes it sounded as though there was someone laughing in the wind. It was a nasty, high pitched laugh. Toots pulled her jacket close around her and shivered again.

She should have been enjoying her Easter holidays, but she wasn't. Toots couldn't wait for them to be over. She couldn't wait to be back at school. She kicked the ground with her toe and set the swing in motion. The days were long and boring. She had no one to play with and nothing to do. Toots could have played with Jemma from across the road, but Jemma was the last person in the world she wanted to see. Toots scowled. The wind screamed louder and the mocking high pitched laugh echoed through the garden.

Jemma had been Toots's best friend, but not anymore. Jemma had let Toots down on the day of the car wash and Toots couldn't forgive her. The really annoying thing was that washing cars to make some extra pocket money had been Jemma's idea in the first place. They'd arranged to wash six cars, but on the day Jemma had disappeared and Toots had had to wash all the cars by herself. It took her till tea-time and by that time she was furious.

When Jemma came round the next morning Toots had stood in the doorway with her arms folded and her face full of fury. She'd been so angry that she didn't even notice that Jemma's eyes were red.

'You're a bit late,' she said sarcastically. 'Where were you when you were needed?'

'I can't tell you,' Jemma replied.

'Jemma?' called a woman's voice. Jemma swung round anxiously and waved to her mother who stood by the car in the street. Jemma looked back at Toots.

'I've got to go. I'll explain everything later, honestly.'

But Toots hadn't been interested in later. As far as she'd been concerned there wouldn't be any 'later'. She'd been furious. Toots had very strict views on friendship. You weren't supposed to let your friends down, you weren't supposed to keep secrets from them and you weren't supposed to break promises. Three very simple rules and Jemma had broken all of them without a word of explanation. Toots would never forgive her.

After that Toots behaved just as though Jemma had never existed. She wouldn't see her, or speak to her, or walk to school with her, or call for her at her house. Several times Jemma called for Toots asking if they could play together, but Toots would hardly say two words and was so rude that Jemma soon gave up.

So now Toots sat on the swing watching the clouds race by and trying not to think about Jemma. Instead she focused her attention on the horse chestnut tree. There was something so sad about it. It should have been in bud, but it wasn't. There wasn't a new leaf in sight and the bare branches reached out forlornly across the April sky as though they were searching for spring.

And it wasn't just the tree, the whole garden was still bare. There weren't any spring flowers even though she and her father had planted hundreds. In all the other gardens on their street, buds were already open and daffodils were nodding beneath the trees, but in Toots's garden there wasn't a crocus, nor a daffodil, nor a tulip, nor a hyacinth to be seen.

Toots's father had been so worried about the garden that he'd asked Mr Phelps, the tree surgeon, to come and take a look at it. Toots had stood beside her father while Mr Phelps, a tall man with a long red nose and bright eyes, had carefully examined the roots, trunk, branches, and twigs of the horse chestnut tree.

He'd jabbed his stick into the soil at the foot of the tree and stared hard into the hole he'd made. His sharp blue eyes seemed to burn right into the earth as though he could see right through the hard brown dirt to the layers below.

'It's strange, this tree's dying all right,' he'd said patting the trunk with the flat of his hand. 'And its roots must be poisoning the whole garden. That's why nothing's coming up anywhere.'

'Can you do something to save the tree?' Toots's dad had asked.

But Mr Phelps had shaken his head. 'I'm afraid it'll have to come down and the sooner the better. I can come over at the end of the week if you like, though it'll be a crime to lose such a beauty.'

'Yes, it will,' Toots's father had sighed as he stared up into the lattice of dark twigs. Toots had slipped her small cold hand inside her father's and given his fingers a squeeze. He'd squeezed hers back and smiled. It was one of his 'don't worry' smiles, but she'd been able to tell he was upset.

Now, sitting on the swing, Toots tried to imagine what the garden would look like when the magnificent tall tree was gone. It would leave such a terrible blank space. Toots remembered how the tree looked every other spring with its new green leaves as big as dishcloths hanging out to dry. She remembered the blossoms fat as church candles that swayed in the summer breeze and the huge conkers which fell all over the lawn in autumn. She always had the best conkers at school and plenty to share, but next autumn she wouldn't have any.

She started to swing and as she climbed higher she could almost touch the branches with her toe. It was one of her favorite games. She could never quite reach. Maybe next year when she'd grown . . . but next year there wouldn't be a tree. Toots stopped trying to reach the branches and let the swing slow down.

'If only,' she thought, looking at the bleak, wintry garden, 'if only there was some way to save the tree.' But Mr Phelps was going to come and chop it down tomorrow afternoon.

The sound of someone scratching at the back door made Toots look up. Binky wanted to come out. Binky was Mrs Willets's dog and he accompanied her every day when she came to look after Toots. Toots's mother had died a long time ago and she was used to other people looking after her during the holidays. With a sigh Toots got off the swing to let Binky into the garden.

Binky was small with short red fur. He looked about a hundred years old because one of his eyes was cloudy and white. Toots didn't much care for him. He would never fetch sticks when she threw them for him and he was always digging holes in the garden. Whenever you took your eyes off him, Binky would be starting a fresh hole in the lawn. Binky's holes were everywhere, except in the patio of crazy paving by the house which Toots's father had made last month.

As for Mrs Willets, she was as wrinkled as a raisin and her black hair was streaked with grey. She wasn't much of a one for playing or going out anywhere. She liked to watch television all day. The minute Toots's father left for work, PING! on went the television and on it stayed till he came home. Every morning Mrs Willets made sandwiches for Toots's lunch so that she didn't have to get up in the middle of one of her programmes. Toots often ate her sandwiches by herself or with Binky, who would oblige her by eating the crusts.

Toots opened the back door and Binky scuttled out into the garden barking happily, Toots pulled a face at him and climbed back on the swing. Binky immediately began to dig in the flowerbeds and with a groan, Toots jumped off the swing and pulled him away.

'Stop it!' she cried. 'Bad dog! That's not allowed!' But Binky already had his nose down a hole and was fighting hard to keep it there. With an enormous effort Toots won and, fixing his lead to his collar, tied the free end to the leg of the swing. She commanded him to stay. Binky lay on the ground with his nose stretched as close as possible to the nearest hole, sniffing and whimpering while Toots returned to the swing and did her best to ignore him.

Suddenly Binky barked once, then rolled over and lay very still with his paws dangling over his chest. He looked daft. One ear was flopped inside out and his eyes flitted back and forth as though he was watching something that only he could see. Toots grew curious. What was he watching? She cocked her head and looked sideways at the broad tree trunk. Nothing seemed out of the ordinary. She leaned further over, but still couldn't see anything.

Binky barked again and wagged his tail with great excitement. Toots sat up and watched him and then, determined to get to the bottom of the mystery, she clung to the swing's ropes and leaned all the way forward until her head was down between her legs and she was looking at the garden and the rest of the world upside down.

A tiny blue creature no bigger than an ant was standing on the underside of the swing. Toots narrowed her eyes. There was something very familiar about this tiny creature, but she couldn't quite put her finger on what it was. Then the creature lifted what looked like a minute megaphone to her lips. Toots suddenly remembered everything and she gasped as all her memories of the Upside Down World came flooding back.

'Olive!' she cried before the tiny creature had had a chance to say a word. 'Olive, is it really you?'

CHAPTER TWO

~ Downside Up Again ~

'Well, thank heavens,' called Olive Brown through the megaphone. 'I've been calling for you all morning, Toots. I thought you were never going to hear me. If it wasn't for your friend over there,' she nodded at Binky, 'I don't think you'd ever have thought to look beneath the swing.'

'Olive?' whispered Toots blushing. 'Oh Olive, I don't know why, but until just now I think I'd forgotten you, I'd forgotten the Upside Down World, I'd forgotten everything.'

'I know, that's what happens,' Olive sighed. 'You can't help it. You just forget all about us, but not to worry, the important thing is that you've seen me now and I've got so much to tell you. Something terrible is happening. Look.'

Olive pointed towards the garden and for the first time Toots noticed what it looked like upside down. It was a shock. A strange white dust covered the underside of every plant in the flowerbeds. The dust lay as thick as snow on the branches of the horse chestnut tree, it gathered in drifts beneath every rock and pebble, and it filled each crevice and nook in the garden. It made the garden look as though all the trees and plants were still buried deep in winter. The white powder covered the underside of the swing and came up as far as Olive's knees. Even the air was full of the white feathery flakes that swirled in the wind. And as the wind blew, the dust rose up in little flurries, then settled down again.

Toots lifted her head. From right ways up you couldn't see any of the snowy dust at all. She turned upside down again.

'I think you might be able to help us,' cried Olive through the megaphone. 'Will you come and try?'

'Of course,' Toots replied, but then she stopped. 'I'll have to be back before my father gets home.'

'You will be. I promise,' replied Olive.

'All right, what shall I do?'

Olive paused for a moment. 'Well, I'll have to bring you to the Upside Down Garden. Let me think, I've never done this outside before. It could be tricky, but I think if you could kneel on the swing and hold on to the seat, that should do it.'

As Toots tried to kneel on the swing, the seat swayed precariously beneath her, even though she did her best to steady it. Toots wasn't at all sure if she was doing the right thing, but she had said that she'd go and she didn't want to break her word. She took a deep breath, bent over forwards and grabbed the wooden seat with both hands.

'Oh, wait a minute,' cried Olive. 'I almost forgot the most important bit.' She flew off the edge of the swing and quickly tied a length of fine cobweb about Toots's wrist. 'I'll need this to pull you up and it'll act as a safety rope just in case you . . . well . . . you know . . . it could be tricky when your gravity switches over, that is when everything that was up becomes down and vice versa. When that happens you mustn't let go of the swing. If you do, your weight might pull us both into the sky and that would be disastrous.'

Toots stared at the sky and shuddered. Safety rope or not, the thought of falling forever terrified her.

'Ready?' asked Olive as she unravelled the cobweb rope.

Toots gulped, then nodded. 'Ready,' she replied, though in truth she didn't really know if she was ready or not.

Olive took a deep breath and yanked on the rope. Toots felt it tug at her wrist and a moment later noticed that the wooden seat was growing thicker. In another moment it was too big for her to grasp and she had to let go with her thumb and could only hold on with her fingers. She shifted her knees and the swing juddered. Olive stumbled.

'Careful!' cried Olive.

'Sorry,' whispered Toots.

Soon Toots could tell she was getting smaller. The swing grew bigger beneath her knees and as the wood thickened, she had to keep adjusting her grip. As it grew, the wood became rough and full of large splits and splinters. Toots peeped over the edge of the seat at Olive.

It was lovely to see Olive's big, red, friendly face again. Olive was wearing a new uniform now, a shimmering, metallic-blue flying suit and a matching helmet with thick straps that fastened under her chin. Her pretty gossamer wings fluttered behind her back. The whole effect was very smart and made her look like a large bluebottle. Toots guessed that it was probably some sort of camouflage.

Toots was overjoyed to see her friend again, but she couldn't shake the feeling that Olive looked a little out of sorts, not cross exactly, but worried and fretful.

Over by the tree she could see the other fairies, in their bluebottle uniforms, flying frantically through the blizzard. They seemed to be snatching at the feathery flakes and trying to put them into their buckets. Toots could see that this was a hopeless task for there were far too many flakes and nowhere near enough fairies and besides, every time they caught hold of a flake, it seemed that they could only hold on to it for a moment before it escaped into the air.

Toots was thinking about this and not concentrating on what she was doing when, with a sudden and incredible jolt, her gravity switched.

All at once the world turned upside down for Toots. She screamed as her legs fell from under her and she found herself hanging with her feet dangling dangerously down towards the sky.

'You'll have to hold on, Toots,' cried Olive trying to pull up on the cobweb rope. 'You're still too heavy. I can't take all your weight. Don't let go of the swing or you'll pull us both down.'

Toots gritted her teeth. Every moment she found it harder to hold on to the expanding swing. It was like trying to cling to the edge of an impossibly high cliff using only the very tips of your fingers, and to make it worse her fingers were shrinking. In truth it was even more difficult than that, because at least a cliff edge would have stayed still. Toots's shift in gravity had made the wooden swing rock so violently that she could do nothing to stop her fingers from slipping. It was only a matter of moments before the inevitable happened. Suddenly she fell. Toots screamed again for all she was worth as she plummeted towards the sky.

'Toots!' cried Olive as the cobweb rope sped

through her fingers. Olive grabbed it and winced as the rope burned her hands. She dug her heels into the swing, flapped her wings furiously and pulled back with all her strength, but Toots's falling weight was too much for her and she was soon dragged right across the wooden seat.

Luckily, just before Olive reached the edge of the swing, the cobweb rope caught fast in one of the large splinters at the edge of the seat. Toots jerked to a stop and cried out in pain. It felt as though her arm was going to be pulled out of its socket.

Olive quickly secured her end of the rope around a nail head and hurried to the edge.

'Toots,' she shouted. 'Do you have the strength to climb up the rope?'

'I think so,' replied Toots and slowly shifting her weight from one hand to the other she hoisted herself up the thin rope towards the swing. When she reached the huge wooden seat she looked up and saw Olive leaning over the edge holding her hand out towards her.

'That's it, just a little further,' Olive smiled and grabbed Toots's hand. A moment later Toots lay deep in the thick white powder on the underside of the swing trying to recover her breath.

'That was close,' puffed Olive as she untied the rope from Toots's wrist and wound the cobweb into a neat coil. Toots sat up and stared across the garden and at the house which loomed in the distance. She picked up a handful of the white powder and found that it wasn't a powder at all, but thousands of small white feathery seed carriers like those from a dandelion clock.

'What is this stuff?' she asked, tossing a handful into the air.

'Don't disturb it,' cried Olive anxiously. 'We're trying to keep it under control.' She picked up a tiny feather. 'These are the furzeweed seed heads. See, most are harmless, because we've already removed the seeds.' Olive shuddered and snatched up another feather. 'But look, here's one that got away.' She plucked a tiny seed off the feathery stalk and put it in her bucket. 'It's nearly an impossible task. And you can see from the state of the garden that there's very little time.'

Toots ran her hands through the dust and found another seed head which was still intact. She yanked the seed from its feather and stared at the tiny pearl in her palm.

'Does this have something to do with why the plants won't grow?' she asked. 'Is this why the garden is dying?'

'Partly,' replied Olive in a distant voice. 'But I don't think we're ever going to beat it this way. We have to get to the root of the problem if we're going to save the garden.' Olive fell silent and seemed to stare at something very far away.

'Olive?' Toots touched her friend on the arm.

'Oh,' Olive blinked and smiled at Toots. 'Come on, the Group Captain will be waiting for us and we'd better hurry if I'm to get you back in time.' And with that she set off briskly across the swing.

Toots looked for somewhere to put the furzeweed seed and, finding nowhere suitable, dropped it into her pocket and hurried after Olive.

'Good, it looks like you've stopped shrinking,' said Olive staring down at Toots. 'I should be able to carry you now. I'll fly as steadily as I can, but I hope you don't get airsick.'

Toots shook her head.

'Olive, am I smaller than the last time you brought me to the Upside Down World?' asked Toots as she looked down at herself.

'Of course you are,' replied Olive as though this was the most ridiculous question. 'Garden fairies are always smaller than House Fairies, in the same way that River Fairies are smaller than the Garden Fairies and Sky Fairies are smaller than everyone. The highest ranked fairies are the smallest of all. It stands to reason. I've been shrinking ever since I graduated from the house to the garden, can't you tell?'

Toots looked up at her friend. To her mind Olive

seemed just as portly as ever, but she didn't want to appear rude or dispute what Olive said so she smiled and nodded in agreement.

Olive tapped her finger against her chin. 'I don't think a standing start's a good idea. It'll be best if you start running, then I'll fly over and pick you up. How does that sound?'

It sounded dangerous, but Toots had promised to try and help and she knew she couldn't back out now. She didn't want to be a promise breaker. She didn't want to let her friend down. She didn't want to be like Jemma. And as this thought crossed her mind, the wind blew more violently across the garden and Toots heard the sinister laugh she'd heard before.

'What's that noise?' she asked anxiously.

'What noise?' answered Olive.

'That strange laughter. . .' Toots stopped. The wind had stilled and the garden was silent. 'It's gone now.'

Olive gave Toots a strange look. 'I didn't hear anything,' she said, shaking her head. 'Come on, let's go,' she urged, nudging Toots.

Toots nodded and began to run as fast as she could through the seed heads. She wasn't even halfway across the swing before she felt Olive's strong arms loop around her middle and lift her up towards the garden.

Toots gasped as they flew upside down across the garden. Flying was wonderful. Below them the sky was full of fat clouds, some white, some gold. Above them the garden lay stark and bare and full of winter.

Olive flew swiftly, circling over the crazy paving with its oddly coloured tiles, then past the fish pond with its bright mirror reflecting the sky, and on towards the horse chestnut tree. They soon passed all the other fairies who were busily filling the buckets at their belts with the tiny white seeds.

Olive swooped around the tree, but just as they came to the far side, Toots looked up and from her upside down viewpoint saw Binky break free from his leash and come bounding across the grass towards them. The fairies scattered.

'That dog's a menace,' said Toots.

'Oh no, he doesn't mean any harm,' laughed Olive as she veered to the left. 'He just wants to play. You see, when he's right side up he can smell us but he can't see us and if we don't get out of the way, he might bash into someone accidentally.'

Toots wasn't convinced. Olive laughed again then veered sharply up towards a dark hole between the tree's roots. On one side there was a long dark scar shaped like the number three.

In an instant they flew inside the dark tunnel and the day disappeared behind them. Toots looked back and saw the tip of Binky's snout crammed into the hole. 'So that's why he was always digging,' she thought. 'He knew there was something down here.'

The tunnel was dark, but Toots didn't feel frightened. She was with Olive and she felt safe, the way you always feel with an old friend.

Far ahead of them there was a light which grew brighter as they approached. Toots could see now that they were not alone in the tunnel. Other fairies flew past them in the darkness and Toots could hear the drone of their wings close by.

'Almost there,' shouted Olive above the echoing drone of so many fluttering wings, and no sooner had she said this than they burst into a large vaulted cave with smooth curved walls. Stretching out before them were two long runways with different coloured blinking lights along the edges. It was all go. Fairies were taking off from one runway and landing on the other. At the far end of the room fairies in orange overalls held up small orange paddles like table tennis bats, and waved them to signal to the incoming flyers.

'When I get close to the runway,' yelled Olive. 'Drop your feet down and as soon as they touch the ground start running. Ready?'

'Ready!' Toots replied.

But the ground rose up so quickly that it took her by surprise and Toots didn't have time to start running. As Olive let go of her and her feet touched the runway, her legs collapsed beneath her like wet straws. Luckily a small red-haired fairy saw her start to fall. She reached out quickly and caught Toots's hands and kept her upright until she came safely to a stop. In all the commotion Toots didn't notice the small white seed fall out of her pocket and bounce across the floor as she landed. Neither did anyone else.

Toots was embarrassed about her botched attempt at a clean landing and it was humiliating to be rescued by someone who looked so young and was obviously a very junior fairy. Nevertheless Toots didn't forget her manners.

'Thank you,' she said.

'It was nothing,' smiled the small fairy. 'You must be Toots. I've heard a lot about . . .' But suddenly the small fairy broke off, her eyes widening in horror.

'Loose seed!' she cried pointing at the small white dot on the runway.

Everyone looked. The seed was turning yellow. A dark circle appeared around it like a damp, oily stain and it was spreading rapidly. Toots felt in her pocket and realized with dismay it was the seed that she'd picked up. Suddenly Olive was at Toots's side, but before Toots could ask her what was happening a deep voice silenced everyone in the room.

'Clear the runways,' it bellowed. Toots turned and saw the largest, most ferocious looking fairy she had ever seen. She was twice as tall as Olive and twice as fat.

Her eyebrows were so thick and bushy that they ran in one straight line across her face. 'Everybody back!' she roared. 'It's only one seed, we should be able to control it. Do not panic!'

As all the fairies hurried to the edges of the room, Olive grabbed Toots by the arm and pulled her out of the way. Within seconds the runways were clear. Everybody waited and watched in absolute silence.

The greasy circle around the small white seed darkened and grew bigger, then with a soft plop the seed sank into the ground and disappeared like a stone in water. Everyone held their breath and watched as the dark circle pulsated.

Suddenly a fairy flew into the cavern from the tunnel and descended towards the runway.

'Turn around, Madeleine!' all the fairies cried. 'Go back! Don't land, Maddy!' But it was too late.

With a great crack the dark circle split and a sharp green thorn shot out of the ground and pierced the room, burying its dagger-like tip in the ceiling. Madeleine screamed, as one of the thorn's sharp barbs caught in the handle of her bucket. It carried her up and pinned her against the ceiling.

'Oh no!' whispered Olive. 'Please let that bucket be empty. Please, please, please.'

The thorn stopped growing and Madeleine dangled helplessly. With an effort she steadied herself and the bucket at her belt. For a moment it seemed as though everything was going to be all right, but then the thorn jerked and jabbed itself further into the ceiling. Madeleine rocked forward and her bucket tipped over. Hundreds upon hundreds of the small white seeds spilled out and skittered across the ground like marbles on glass. It was a disaster.

'Red alert!' bellowed the huge fairy. 'Everybody out! We have to seal this room immediately.' And with that she hit a large button on the wall and an alarm began to wail.

Everyone rushed towards the big metal doors.

'Go that way,' shouted Olive, pushing Toots along with the crowd. 'I won't be long. I have to help Madeleine.' Olive sprang into the air and flew towards the fairy on the thorn who was now in tears.

Toots hurried along with the fairies, but at the door she turned and looked back. Olive had already freed the trapped fairy and was helping her down. The hangar was almost empty, save for the thick green thorn which speared the room at its centre and the hundreds of yellowing seeds on the floor. One by one the seeds disappeared into the ground. Then within seconds the thick green thorns sprouted up one after another, driving their pointed tips deep into the ceiling.

'Out of the way there,' bellowed the huge fairy, tugging roughly on Toots's shoulder. 'This room has to be sealed. Step back.'

Toots wanted to say 'wait for Olive', but the words dried up in her mouth when she saw the huge fairy glowering down at her. Toots hurried through the doors to get out of her way.

From the corridor Toots watched desperately for Olive and wished there was something she could do to help. She stared at the tangle of furzeweed in the landing bay and as she stared, a chill ran over her heart. She could see something hidden deep within the thorns. It was a face, or rather part of a face, and one evil yellow eye as thin and as cold as the new moon was staring back at her. This hideous eye seemed to be laughing. Its pupil was as beady and black as a crab's, and it danced in the yellow slit. Beneath the eye a long dark gash opened up across the face where the mouth should have been. It was like a wound. Toots shivered, but she couldn't look away. She looked deeper and deeper into that yellow eye and took an involuntary step towards the door. She would have gone further, but suddenly she saw Olive pushing through the thorns with the fairy Madeleine clinging to her back. The yellow eye and evil mouth rippled like a reflection in a pond and vanished into the thorns.

Toots blinked, then roused herself. Olive's face was blotched with pink, her helmet had fallen to the back of her head and her eyes looked wild. Toots rushed to help her friend.

'Thanks,' said Olive as Toots helped her carry Madeleine through the door.

'Come on, out of the way,' bawled the big fairy. Olive and Toots hurried into the corridor, and as soon as they were clear, the huge fairy slammed the doors to the landing bay shut, then leaned heavily against them and slid all the bolts in place.

'I'm sorry,' cried Madeleine, her whole frame shaking with big heart-wrenching sobs.

'Humph! No use crying over it now, is there?' was all that the huge fairy said as she placed two sturdy bars across the doors and made sure they were secure. 'Landing Bay Number Three is now out of service,' she croaked, blowing her nose noisily. 'Everyone back to Garden Squadron HQ at the double.'

'Who is that?' asked Toots in a whisper.

'Our Wing Commander,' replied Olive. 'She's wonderful, but she's not happy at the moment. It's the third landing bay we've lost this week. At this rate all our exits will soon be sealed and we'll be trapped down here forever.'

'Olive, why can't I see the furzeweed in the garden?'

'Because unlike most plants, furzeweed grows down instead of up. It burrows deep into the ground and chokes a garden from beneath.'

'Does it have a face?'

Olive stopped a moment and looked at Toots.

'Not that I've heard of,' said Olive. 'Why?'

'I thought I . . . oh nothing, no reason,' answered Toots. She didn't want to tell Olive that she thought she'd seen a face amongst the thorns, it seemed silly.

'Come on,' said Olive giving Toots's shoulder a friendly nudge. 'We've got to get to the Group Captain.'

'Is she like the Wing Commander?' asked Toots fearfully.

'Oh no, she's much sterner,' said Olive with a smile. 'Come on.'

Toots gulped and followed her friend.

CHAPTER THREE

~ The Group Captain ~

'Come on, we must hurry,' urged Olive, pulling on Toots's wrist for the umpteenth time.

The pale green corridor was packed with bustling fairies, but Olive still managed to move quickly, weaving through the crowd like a swift boat in a busy shipping lane. Toots had to trot to keep up.

But she didn't always want to keep up. There was so much to see. Every few yards Toots stopped and tried to peek into the rooms which lay beyond the glass panelled doors on either side of the corridor. Every time she stopped, Olive tugged at her wrist and dragged her away before she could really see anything at all. Every time she stopped, Olive tugged at her wrist and hurried her away. They went so quickly that Toots only caught fleeting glances of the intricately detailed maps that hung along the corridor, only the merest glimpse of a classroom blackboard covered in arrows showing 'Wind Directions for April', and hardly anything at all of a fascinating room where fairies were pushing little model plants across a large table-top painting of the garden. All of these looked intriguing and she would have loved to hang around and ask all sorts of nosey questions, but she didn't get a chance because Olive was in no mood to dally.

Eventually they stopped by a large door with a sliding glass hatch.

'Here's the Group Captain's office,' Olive whispered, trying to straighten her flying suit and tuck her unruly hair into her helmet. 'Ready?' she asked. Toots nodded and Olive rapped smartly on the glass.

In an instant the glass hatch slid open and the Wing Commander's big scowling face appeared.

'Is that her?' she demanded, thrusting her chin towards Toots. Toots shrank back against Olive.

'Yes, ma'am. This is Toots.'

'Humph! Humans! They're usually the ones who cause all the trouble! I suppose you'd better bring her in. And she'd better be as good as you say.'

The Wing Commander slammed the hatch shut and Olive had barely enough time to whisper, 'Don't mind her, she's just a bit gruff. It's said that she once had a very bad experience with a human. . .' before the door flew open and the Wing Commander glared down at them.

Olive fell quiet and Toots instinctively shrank back

again as the Wing Commander thrust out her big hand. Toots didn't understand what was expected of her until Olive nudged her and she realized that the Wing Commander only wanted to shake hands. Toots held out her hand and the Wing Commander shook it so firmly that for a moment she thought her fingers would drop off.

'Pleased to meet you,' mumbled the Wing Commander in a not very convincing manner. 'The Group Captain is waiting for you,' she added gruffly. 'Just go in. Brown, you know the way.'

'Yes, thank you, ma'am. Come on, Toots,' Olive led Toots through a small outer office, knocked on the door at the far end, opened it and ushered Toots inside.

Toots entered a large cosy room full of furniture and overflowing bookshelves. It was so crowded that there was hardly an inch of carpet to be seen, and most of the space was taken by an enormous wooden desk which was covered in papers and books.

It was some time before Toots noticed that the little red-headed fairy, who earlier had saved her from a nasty fall, was standing on a stool by the desk. The fairy had her nose buried in a book and she was lost deep in thought. Toots wondered what the junior flyer could be doing in the Group Captain's office looking through the Group Captain's things and hoped that she wouldn't get into trouble when the Group Captain returned.

Olive coughed politely and the little fairy looked up.

'Ma'am, may I introduce Toots? Toots, this is our Group Captain.'

'Oh . . . ' stammered Toots, opening and closing her mouth like a fish.

'I'm very pleased to meet you,' said the Group Captain, smiling.

Toots was so surprised that for a moment she couldn't bring herself to say anything at all. How could someone so young and so small be in charge of a whole squadron of fairies? It seemed ridiculous.

Toots was speechless, but luckily she didn't have to say anything because just then there was a knock at the door and the Wing Commander entered carrying a dainty tea tray in her big, paw-like hands.

'Thought you might like a spot of refreshment, ma'am,' she said.

'Thank you, Wing Commander Lewis,' replied the little fairy. 'What's the latest report?'

'Landing Bay Number Three is now confirmed inoperative, ma'am.'

The Group Captain shook her head, reached over to a map on the desk and drew a red cross by the foot of the horse chestnut tree.

'We have to find a way to stop this,' she whispered to herself. Then she looked up. 'Lewis, please stay while I brief Toots on the situation.'

'Yes, ma'am,' replied Wing Commander Lewis casting a disapproving eye in Toots's direction.

The young Group Captain sat on the edge of her desk with her legs dangling and motioned for Olive and Toots to make themselves comfortable. Toots sat in an armchair which was covered in books and Olive perched on the arm.

The Group Captain clasped her tiny hands together on her lap and began.

'Well, Toots, it was Olive's idea that we bring you here. She thought that you might be able to help.'

'Humph,' coughed the Wing Commander.

The Group Captain ignored her and carried on. 'We've all heard about your bravery in the Upside Down House and how it was your ingenuity that saved the house from the evil forces of Jack Frost.' Toots blushed. What the Group Captain said was true, but that episode had had many twists and turns and Toots could not think of it without a twinge of shame.

The Group Captain went on. 'Today, Toots, you saw the damage the thorny furzeweed can cause. You saw how it invades and destroys the garden by burrowing down and choking the soil. If the furzeweed is allowed to take over the garden, all the plants and even the horse chestnut tree, which has stood so long, will die.'

'The horse chestnut tree?' Toots half whispered to herself. 'But Mr Phelps said that the tree was already dead. He's going to chop it down.'

'What? Who's going to chop it down?' cried Olive, overhearing Toots's whispers.

'Chop it down? When?' demanded the Wing Commander, spilling her tea.

'He's coming tomorrow afternoon,' answered Toots.

'Hah!' bellowed the Wing Commander, rattling her teacup. 'Typical of humans. The tree isn't even dead and they want to cut it down.'

'We don't want to,' protested Toots. 'But Mr Phelps, the tree surgeon, says if it isn't cut down, the whole garden will die.'

'The tree's not the problem!' snapped the Wing Commander with such ferocity that Toots rocked back against Olive.

The Group Captain held up her hand to silence the Wing Commander who sat back grumpily. The Group Captain turned back to Toots and tried to smile, but her eyes were full of sorrow.

'Tomorrow, you say?' She waited while Toots confirmed this. 'Then there's less time than we thought. You see, the furzeweed is not our only problem. If it was, we wouldn't need your help so desperately.' Here she paused and looked Toots in the eye. 'No, I'm afraid our problem is far greater. You see, something is making the furzeweed stronger than it should be. Something is using it to take over and destroy the garden.'

The Group Captain paused again and took a deep breath.

'I'm afraid we have a Waspgnat in the garden and unless we can find a way to defeat it, the garden will die.'

The Group Captain stopped speaking and a deep and terrible silence descended upon the three fairies. Toots was reluctant to be the first to speak, but she had to know. She mustered all her courage and asked in a whisper, 'What is a Waspgnat? How did it get here?'

The three fairies looked at each other.

'Well,' began Olive in a halting voice, 'a Waspgnat is a Garden Fairy's greatest fear. No one knows what one looks like, because no fairy who has seen a Waspgnat's face has ever returned to tell the tale. A Waspgnat leaves no survivors. It devours its prisoners and turns them into wraiths, and wraiths can't speak.'

'Nobody knows where a Waspgnat comes from,' added the Group Captain. 'But everyone knows that no garden in living memory has ever survived one.'

Then the Wing Commander began to speak in a low voice. 'Some say that a Waspgnat can be brought on by something or someone. And it's that someone's bad feeling, bitterness, resentment and anger that can make the Waspgnat grow and get stronger. . .'

The Group Captain coughed loudly and knocked a book off the desk.

'Now, now,' she said, with a hard meaningful stare at the Wing Commander. 'You know that's just an old tale.'

The Wing Commander instantly fell quiet and glowered at the floor.

'I've never even heard of a Waspgnat,' said Toots to lighten the mood.

The Wing Commander looked up sharply. 'That's not surprising,' she snapped. 'It's not the sort of thing they teach in your schools. Very few humans would know what a Waspgnat was if it was lying on their lawn. And it's not even as though humans can't see them, you don't even have to be upside down.'

'But how can it destroy a garden?' asked Toots.

'A Waspgnat is a terrible thing,' said the Group Captain, hopping down off the desk. 'As soon as a Waspgnat invades a garden, all the creatures and insects leave. Spring will not come. Plants and trees wither and die. Any creatures who do not leave behave contrary to their nature. Ants will not work, bees will not buzz, worms will not wriggle. Sometimes the influence of the Waspgnat has spread so far that insects start to talk and act quite like humans, giving themselves names and airs and graces. And then everything goes to pot.' The Group Captain quickly leafed through the pages of a book on her desk. 'And it says here that Waspgnats are devilishly hard to find. They can roam all over the garden and hide anywhere. The longer they stay, the more powerful they become until they are impossible to destroy, and then the garden is done for.'

'I knew a garden once that had a Waspgnat,' said the Wing Commander sadly. 'None of us could do anything to stop it. It was using nettles then, not furzeweed. The whole garden was soon nothing but nettles. That was a very unhappy time. A very unhappy. . .' The Wing Commander stopped and blew her nose noisily.

'That won't happen here,' said the Group Captain gently. 'If Toots can't come up with anything, we'll leave immediately. We won't let any of our fairies become wraiths, I promise.'

'But if you leave, you'll lose the garden,' cried the Wing Commander. 'And they'll never give you another.'

The Group Captain nodded, then walked to where Toots sat and looked her straight in the eye.

'There is only one way to save the garden. We must find a way to defeat the Waspgnat. Will you help us?'

Toots didn't have a clue how to defeat a Waspgnat, but she didn't want to let Olive or the Group Captain down.

'What do you want me to do?'

The Group Captain looked at her steadily.

'Because of the Waspgnat, the furzeweed that is

invading the garden is growing ten times faster and twenty times stronger than normal. We need you to help us find something that will break the death grip the furzeweed is gaining over the garden. If we can break this, it might buy us some time, perhaps enough for us to find a way to defeat the Waspgnat.'

Toots frowned and tried to look as though she was thinking hard, but she didn't have even an inkling.

'What's the use?' muttered the Wing Commander.

Toots's frown deepened. She knew she wasn't stupid, but she couldn't think of anything. Then she had an idea. It wasn't the idea that she was searching for, it didn't have anything to do with the Waspgnat, but it was an idea.

'I think. . .' she began quietly and the three fairies leaned in close to hear. 'I think I might be able to think of something if I had a little time.'

The Wing Commander threw up her hands in disgust. 'Time is the one thing we don't have,' she groaned.

'But I have to get back before my father comes home from work,' implored Toots. 'He'll be worried if I'm missing. I promise I'll try and think of something tonight. I might find something in one of my father's books. Or I could ask him.'

'I suppose we can wait for just one night,' said the Group Captain. 'We should give Toots time. It's not fair of us to ask her to think of something on the spot like that. We can wait until tomorrow and hopefully you'll. . . well, hopefully. If Toots can't think of anything, then we'll have to pack up and move out.'

'And lose the garden and the tree?' groaned the Wing Commander.

'Yes, and lose the garden and the tree. We won't have any choice.'

The Wing Commander glared angrily at the floor and not for the first time that afternoon it crossed Toots's mind that the Wing Commander wasn't as full of fairy goodness as she should have been. Toots wondered why. Then it struck her. Perhaps she was jealous of the Group Captain.

'It must be very hard,' she reasoned, 'for the Wing Commander to take orders from someone as small and as young as the Group Captain. Maybe that's why she's so ferocious.'

'Very well, Brown,' commanded the Group Captain. 'You'd better take Toots home before it gets too late. I'll see you tomorrow, Toots, bright and as early as you can.'

'I can be here by half past eight,' said Toots remembering that Mrs Willets would spend the whole day in front of the television.

'Very good. We'll call a squadron meeting for a quarter to nine.'

And with that the Group Captain returned to the book on her desk and was soon lost in thought.

'You'll have to use Landing Bay Number Five,' barked the Wing Commander as she led Olive and Toots to the door. 'It's still operational. And tomorrow you'd better make sure that you have all loose seed heads under control. We don't want a repeat of today's performance.'

Toots shrank a little under the Wing Commander's scowl and felt guilty. Did the Wing Commander know it was Toots who'd dropped the seed on the runway?

CHAPTER FOUR

~ The Search for an Idea ~

Landing Bay Number Five was much smaller than Number Three had been and it was four times as crowded. The air seemed thick with fairies landing and taking off, and all of them looked exhausted. A number of fairies were climbing up high ladders and emptying buckets full of seeds into huge metal drums, some of which bore bright paper labels. After a moment Toots recognized the labels. The drums were old tomato soup and baked bin tins. She was amazed at how big they were.

'I must be tiny,' she thought.

'Right, Toots,' said Olive. 'Get ready to start running. Here we go. Now . . . run!'

And Toots ran. She could hear Olive's thunderous footsteps behind her and then suddenly she couldn't. A moment later she felt Olive pull her into the air and together they flew towards the dark tunnel.

This tunnel veered sharply down and soon Toots

could see the sky below them between the thick bars of a grid. The opening looked dangerously narrow. The other fairies slipped easily between the bars, but they were flying solo, they weren't carrying anyone. How was Olive going to fit through the grate with Toots? Olive flew faster.

'Hold on,' she yelled as they sped towards the narrow exit.

Toots closed her eyes and gripped Olive's arms. Olive twisted sharply to the left and Toots heard the iron grating whistle by, then suddenly felt the fresh wind on her face. She opened her eyes and breathed a sigh of relief. They'd made it. They were flying down towards the sky.

The sun was setting as Olive carried Toots beneath the tops of the rose bushes and swooped down past the sun dial. The light bounced off the pond and golden ripples danced along the fence. Far below them in the sky, a solitary raven flew in lazy circles.

'Shall I leave you where I found you?' asked Olive banking round towards the swing.

Toots was about to answer yes, when the back door opened and Mrs Willets appeared with her hands on her hips.

'Charlotte? Charlotte?' she called in her high pitched voice. 'Time to come in. Your father will be home in a minute.' She stepped out into the garden, rested her hand on the frame of the swing and stood looking puzzled. Binky trotted at her heels and barked at the empty garden.

'You can't drop me by the swing, not with her standing there,' said Toots. 'Can you take me inside the house?'

Olive changed direction and flew towards the open door, but just as they reached it, Toots's father came out. He looked around anxiously when he saw Mrs Willets standing in the garden calling for Toots.

Olive quickly veered to the right and flew up the side of the house.

'My bedroom window's open,' cried Toots. 'Quick, fly in there.'

Toots could hear her father calling for her in the garden.

'Hurry,' she insisted. 'I don't want him to think I'm missing.'

Olive swiftly flew in through the window and landed on the underside of the dressing table. Then she waved her hands and almost immediately Toots began to feel the dressing table start to shrink beneath her feet.

'I'll wait for you by the swing tomorrow morning,' called Olive as she rapidly grew smaller. 'You won't forget to think about our problem, will you?'

'I won't forget,' promised Toots. Olive was just about to fly away when Toots cried, 'Olive? Won't I just forget you like before? How can I remember your problem if I can't remember you?'

Olive's mouth dropped open. 'That's a very good point,' she squeaked. 'Here, catch.' Olive quickly unfastened her bucket from her belt and threw it up to Toots. 'As long as you hold something from the Upside Down World, you'll remember us. Don't lose it, whatever you do.'

'I won't,' cried Toots as she caught the bucket. It was the size of a thimble in her hand and she slipped her little finger inside it and felt it tighten as she grew.

The floor loomed towards her, the swirls on the carpet grew bigger, and her feet soon covered almost half of the underside of the dressing table. There wasn't much room for her to grow. She was already bent double and was quickly running out of space.

Toots reached up and laid her hands flat against the floor and felt her gravity switch back to the normal world where everything that was up was up and all that was down was down. When this happened she fell against the floor and found that she was trapped beneath the dressing table. Now she couldn't move because her head was scrunched up against the carpet, her knees were bent against her chest and her feet were caught against the table. She was stuck fast. She couldn't even shout.

'Help!' she hissed through gritted teeth.

A moment later her bedroom door flew open and Binky rushed in. He pounced on Toots, barking with joy and licking her face and ears. Toots was defenceless and couldn't push him away.

'Help,' Toots spluttered, trying to worm away from the dog's kisses.

'Toots! How on earth did you get yourself stuck like that?' asked her father as he rushed into the room and pulled Binky away.

'I was just playing,' answered Toots. Her father lifted the dressing table out of the way and she rolled to one side.

'You gave us quite a scare, didn't she, Mrs Willets?' he said. 'We thought you'd run away, joined the army or something.'

'Well, what a relief,' gasped Mrs Willets as she fastened Binky's lead to his collar. 'I'll be off then. See you tomorrow.' She pulled her woollen hat over her ears and waddled off down the steps dragging the reluctant dog behind her.

'You looked pretty funny down there,' said Toots's dad. 'Come on, I've brought fish and chips for supper.'

'And mushy peas?'

'Of course. You set the table and I'll serve them out. I got extra in case you wanted to run over the road and invite Jemma.'

'No thanks,' Toots answered without looking at him.

'Toots? Don't you think it's about time you and Jemma. . .'

'No thanks!' Toots hurried down the stairs. She didn't want to talk about Jemma. Just the thought of going round there with a 'peace offering' of fish and chips made her angry and sour. Why couldn't her father understand? She was no longer friends with Jemma. It was that simple.

Toots started to lay the kitchen table, banging down the plates and knives and forks as though that was the only way to get them to stay there. Nothing was going to make her forget how Jemma had let her down. She was never going to forgive her and that was that.

Suddenly the back door blew open and bashed violently against the sink. Toots hurried to close it, but as she pushed it shut, she heard again the hideous mocking laughter screaming in the wind. She closed the door firmly in an effort to shut out the horrible noise.

As Toots turned back to the table, she felt Olive's bucket pinch her little finger and it reminded her that she had a lot of thinking to do before she went to bed.

'Mrs Willets asked me if we could look after Binky for the weekend,' said Toots's father over supper. 'She's got to visit her sister and Binky's not allowed. I said yes, you don't mind, do you?'

'No,' answered Toots, not really listening because

she was thinking about the terrible furzeweed and how the fairies could stop it.

'Dad, what do you know about plants that destroy other plants?' she asked.

'Not much,' her father shrugged. 'But there's a book on gardening on the shelf. That might be of some use. You get started on the washing up and I'll get it for you.'

Toots had almost finished the washing up by the time her father returned.

'There might be something useful here,' he said, handing her a thick brown book.

'Thanks, Dad,' Toots took it to her room and lay on the bed turning the pages. But there were very few pictures and nothing about furzeweed. Toots tried to read through the thick text, but she kept reading the same sentence over and over again until she couldn't see anything but words swimming up in front of her face.

'Maybe I'll get ready for bed first, then I'll feel more like reading,' she thought. She washed herself, then brushed her teeth and put on her pyjamas, but after all this she felt no more in the mood for reading a serious text book than she had before. Still, she had to try. She had promised she would. Toots sat on the bed and opened the book once more, but she couldn't concentrate and soon found herself drifting off.

She began to daydream. It was much easier than

reading, especially when the reading was so difficult and the daydreaming was so pleasant. She started to imagine just how she would feel in the morning when the entire garden squadron was assembled in front of her. Of course they'd all be cheering, because Toots would have saved the garden with her clever, no, her brilliant idea – an idea that only someone as smart and as intelligent as Toots could have had. Toots didn't notice the heavy book slip off the bed and fall to the floor with a thud. She was too busy listening to the fairies in her mind who just cheered louder and louder. Toots smiled as she snuggled down on her pillow. Tomorrow she would save the garden. And with that pleasant thought she dropped happily off to sleep.

CHAPTER FIVE

~ A Secret Mission ~

When she woke up Toots had a nagging feeling that there was something she had forgotten to do, but it wasn't until she felt Olive's bucket pinching her little finger that she remembered. She hadn't thought of an answer to the fairies' problem. She jumped out of bed and threw open the curtains. The air was full of the promise of spring, but there was no sign of it in her garden.

Across the street Toots could see Jemma playing catch by herself. Toots scowled when Jemma looked up and waved shyly. Toots didn't wave back. She just turned her face to the sky and waited until Jemma stopped waving, then with great deliberation she left the window.

Mrs Willets arrived as usual at eight o'clock and as soon as Toots's father had left for the day, she made sandwiches for Toots, then settled herself on the sofa with a cup of tea and the biscuit box, ready to watch the first of her daily programmes.

At a quarter past eight Toots wrapped her sandwiches, which happened to be cheese and pickle, in a brown paper bag then put them in her pocket and went outside to wait for Olive.

While Toots sat on the swing she thought as hard as she could about the fairies' problem. The wind blew through her hair, but it might as well have been blowing right through her head. Time was running out and she still hadn't thought of an answer. The wind rattled and cackled through the fence, but Toots was so wrapped up in her thoughts that she didn't even notice the mocking laughter.

She gazed up at the bare branches of the horse chestnut tree. How could she help the fairies save the garden? Toots didn't know how, she only knew she had to try. She'd promised to try.

She went over everything she'd heard in the Group Captain's office and remembered how the Wing Commander had said that some people believed that Waspgnats are brought to gardens, invited in, encouraged. Something bothered Toots about the way the Group Captain had looked so strange when she'd interrupted the Wing Commander.

Toots wondered if there was any truth in what the Wing Commander had been saying. The Group Captain had dismissed it as just an old story. But sometimes those old stories were true.

Toots gnawed her lip and narrowed her eyes. Perhaps there was some force at work. Perhaps someone had brought the Waspgnat to the garden, but who? It would have to be someone who wanted to see the Group Captain fail, someone who would gain a good deal if that happened, someone who might even get control of the garden. Toots tapped her fingers on her knees. The only person who would gain by such a thing was . . . Toots drew in her breath . . . of course, why hadn't she realised before? It had to be . . . the Wing Commander!

Toots slapped her leg. It was obvious. She had seen for herself how the Wing Commander resented taking orders from the little Group Captain. It wasn't at all difficult to imagine the gruff, over-bearing Wing Commander plotting to get rid of her senior officer so that she could take over the garden.

Toots didn't much care for the Wing Commander. So what if she'd once had a bad experience with a human? That was no reason to be rude to Toots. But perhaps there was another reason. Toots nodded to herself. Maybe the Wing Commander knew that Toots was clever enough to figure out her plan. Perhaps she was afraid that Toots would soon come up with some brilliant idea to save the garden and thereby foil all her ambitions to take over. Perhaps that was why the Wing Commander didn't want Toots around.

The wind shrieked through the fence. Toots jumped at the sound and shook her head. She wondered if she should tell Olive of her suspicions, but what would she say? She had no evidence to prove that the Wing Commander was planning to take over the garden. It was just a feeling, a feeling that there was some truth in the old story. No matter what the Group Captain said, it made sense to Toots that someone or something could have brought the Waspgnat to the garden and she was pretty certain it was the Wing Commander.

Toots glanced at her watch. It was half past eight and there was still no sign of Olive. Toots rolled her eyes. Of course there was no sign of Olive, she couldn't see her unless she was upside down. Toots grabbed the ropes and doubled over. Now she could see it all. There was the white furzeweed dust, there was the tiny silver bucket on her little finger and there was Olive waiting for her on the underside of the swing.

'Good morning,' called Olive. 'Did you come up with something?' Toots couldn't bear to let Olive down by telling her the truth so she nodded and held up her thumb.

'I'll have thought of something by the time I get down there,' she told herself. Toots knelt on the swing and took hold of the seat. This time she made sure she held on tight when her gravity switched and there were no mishaps.

'Well, what's your idea?' asked Olive as she helped Toots onto the bottom of the swing.

But Toots still had no idea. 'If you don't mind,' she began, 'I'd like to tell everyone at once. It's rather complicated.'

Olive gave her a quizzical look. 'We'd better hurry then,' she said and before long the two of them were flying towards the entrance of Landing Bay Number Five.

Toots hardly noticed the flight because she was so worried. Why hadn't she just told Olive the truth? Why had she lied? What was she was going to say to the Group Captain or the fairies? She didn't want to let them down. She desperately wanted to have the answer to their problems. But no matter how much she worried about it, no answer came.

'By the time we reach the grate,' she promised herself, 'I'll have thought of something.' But they reached the grate and flew through it and she hadn't thought of anything at all.

'By the time we fly into the tunnel, I'll have an idea.' But they flew into the tunnel and still nothing.

'By the time we land, I'll have it. I'll know what to do, the answer will come to me.' But even then she still didn't have the answer. She handed Olive back her bucket and wondered what on earth she was going to say to the Group Captain and the Wing Commander when Olive took her to them.

But Olive didn't take Toots into the Group Captain's office. Instead she led her into a large assembly hall which was packed with forty neatly dressed Garden Fairies all standing to attention. Toots was petrified. She couldn't speak to a whole roomful of fairies. She didn't have anything to say. She tugged on Olive's sleeve and tried to whisper that she needed to speak to her in private, but Olive didn't hear her. She merely gave Toots a broad encouraging smile and directed her up on to the platform at the front of the room where the Wing Commander and the Group Captain were waiting. The Wing Commander stepped forward.

'I'd like to say good morning, squadron, but I'm afraid this is not a very good morning. You are all aware of the situation in the garden. The Waspgnat was extremely active earlier today and we suspect that it has increased its strength at least threefold since then.' The Wing Commander paused momentarily to let the squadron absorb this information, then she continued, 'Brown here had the idea that this human child might be able to help us find a way to get rid of the Waspgnat. So let's hear what she has to say.' She threw a ferocious glare at Toots and stepped back.

Toots's knees began to shake as she looked from one expectant face to the next. How could she tell them that she had no great idea, no clever solution, no wonderful answer? Olive smiled at her in encouragement. Toots opened her mouth, but she couldn't make a sound. It was like being caught in a nightmare. She wanted to run away, but her feet felt as though they were stuck to the stage. The hall was deathly quiet. A pin drop would have sounded like thunder. Then suddenly the storm broke.

'Well?' boomed the Wing Commander, shattering the silence.

Toots's cheeks flushed red and her face burned.

'Do you have an answer or not?' the Wing Commander glared down at her.

'I tried to find one, but . . .' answered Toots in a small voice.

The Wing Commander threw up her hands in disgust. 'She's wasting our time!' she declared.

Toots fell silent. She knew she'd messed up horribly. Forty pairs of fairy eyes stared at her sympathetically which made her feel worse. If they'd been angry she could have borne it better. Toots wished that the ground would open up and swallow her, but it didn't.

'I said it was too much to hope that a human would be able to do anything remotely helpful,' muttered Wing Commander Lewis. But the tiny Group Captain stepped out from behind the vast bulk of her second-in-command and gently took hold of Toots's arm. Immediately the Wing Commander sputtered into silence like an old car stalling its engine and all the fairies craned forward to hear what the Group Captain had to say.

'I don't think we should be angry with Toots,' she said gently. 'It wasn't an easy task and I'm sure she tried her best to think of something.'

'Humph!' muttered the Wing Commander, folding her arms and jutting out her chin.

The Group Captain ignored her and turned to the hall full of fairies. 'I'm sorry to have to tell you this, but I'm afraid the time has come. We will have to leave the garden.'

All the fairies groaned with disappointment and murmured amongst themselves, but the Group Captain held up her hand and the fairies fell silent.

'Listen to me very carefully. I want no heroics. No one is to search for the Waspgnat and try to fight it on their own. It will not help us to lose any of you now. The Waspgnat is too strong. I cannot afford to have any of my fairies turned into wraiths. Please remember that. I really am very sorry about this, but we must leave. We have no alternative. All units are to be packed and ready to evacuate the garden by late this afternoon.'

The Group Captain turned away and nodded at the Wing Commander. The huge fairy sniffed loudly, then clapped her hands and bellowed, 'Operation Clear Out is now underway. Let's get to it.'

The fairies waited in their ranks until the Wing Commander and the Group Captain had left, then they broke up into little groups. Ripples of anxious chatter filled the air as the fairies filed out of the room.

'I'm so sorry, Olive,' said Toots, her voice faltering as she sat on the edge of the platform and hung her head. 'I'm sorry I lied to you, but I was so sure that I'd think of something and I didn't want to tell you that I'd failed. I'm sorry I let you down.'

Olive sat beside her. 'Shush. Don't worry and don't blame yourself. It won't do any good. It was kind of you to try and help. But there's nothing to be done now. Come on, I'd better take you home.' Olive stood up and led the way out of the hall.

'What will happen to you when you leave?' she asked. 'Where will you go?'

'We'll be homeless fairies, a garden squadron without a garden. Eventually we'll be split up and re-assigned to other gardens. All except the Group Captain, of course. She'll never be put in charge of another garden. She has to take the responsibility for there being a Waspgnat in this one.'

'That's terrible,' said Toots.

'It is, but it's worse for the garden. If we leave, the Waspgnat will take over and let the furzeweed run amok, then spring will never ever come and nothing will ever grow here.'

'Was what the Wing Commander said true?' asked Toots. 'You know, the old story about someone bringing a Waspgnat to the garden.'

Olive's cheeks flushed red and she turned away from Toots. 'Oh no. No, no, no. Certainly not,' she replied with a forced laugh. 'Oh dear me, no, no.'

After that Olive quickened her pace. Toots frowned and trotted to keep up.

She wanted to ask Olive more questions, but the corridor soon became too crowded. Fairies on ladders were busy unscrewing pictures from the walls and taking down light fittings, while others were packing books into baskets or rolling up maps. It was impossible for Toots to ask Olive anything in such a crush.

Eventually Olive turned down an empty corridor and Toots was able to keep pace, but now she was too out of breath to ask questions. They hadn't gone very far when a door on their right opened a crack.

'Brown,' hissed a voice from within. Olive and Toots stopped. The room beyond was dark and shadowy. 'Brown,' hissed the voice again, 'Come in here. Leave the human where she is.'

'Toots, stay here and wait for me,' said Olive as she slipped inside. Toots peered in after her and recognized the Wing Commander's large face half hidden in the shadows. Then the darkness swallowed Olive up and the door closed behind her.

What did the Wing Commander want with Olive? Toots wondered. Toots made sure that no one was watching, then crouched down and pressed her ear against the door. If she listened hard she could just make out the mumbling voices within.

'I need your help, Brown. You trust me, don't you?'

'Yes, ma'am,' replied Olive.

'The Group Captain doesn't know I'm here,' hissed the Wing Commander. 'She mustn't know. Do you understand?'

'I think so, ma'am.'

Toots frowned. What were they hiding from the Group Captain? She pressed her ear closer to the door. The Wing Commander was whispering again.

'It will be dangerous. Incredibly dangerous. I need you to hunt down the Waspgnat and steal its most precious possession. It's the only way we can save the garden.'

Outside in the corridor Toots now knew that she'd been right to suspect the Wing Commander, for here she was asking Olive to perform some impossibly dangerous task behind the Group Captain's back and telling her it was so that the garden would be saved. But who would control the garden when the Waspgnat was gone, Toots wondered.

The Wing Commander spoke again, this time

quickly as though the words themselves were too dangerous to let hang in the air.

'Everyone thinks that no fairy has ever faced the Waspgnat and survived to tell the tale, but I know of one fairy who did. It happened a long, long time ago, in a garden that was dying just like ours. She didn't save that garden, but she tried, oh she tried. That fairy told me how she had battled the Waspgnat. 'You must never let it get hold of your thoughts,' she told me. 'If you do, you're lost. Once it has your mind, you're already a shadowy wraith. You must close your mind and never let it into your thoughts.'

'But what is it you want me to steal? What is the Waspgnat's most precious possession?' asked Olive in a trembling voice.

'Shush,' whispered the Wing Commander cutting her off. 'You must remember that the Waspgnat will be listening out for your thoughts. Once you leave this room you must never repeat what I am going to tell you. You must not even think about it, or you'll give the game away.'

The Wing Commander was silent for a moment, then she went on.

'That fairy also told me about the secret of the Waspgnat's power. This is what she'd been trying to find when she was captured and tortured by the Waspgnat.' The Wing Commander's voice sank even lower. 'The Waspgnat holds a purple stone, here, in its chest. It's called the Olm and as the Waspgnat increases in strength, the Olm grows bigger. This is what I need you to steal and destroy, then, and only then, will we be able to save the garden.

'But just stealing the Olm does not kill the Waspgnat. Once you have the stone you must find a way to destroy it as quickly as possible. If you do not, the Waspgnat will quickly bury itself deep in the garden and start to grow another. If this happens, there'll be no hope for any of us.

'Don't look so worried,' continued the Wing Commander in a strangely gentle voice. 'We are lucky, we have one advantage. The Waspgnat has no idea that any fairy knows about the secret of its power. It will not know that you are seeking the Olm. As long as we have this advantage, we have a chance. This is why you must not breathe a word or even think about your mission beyond this room.

'Olive, you are the best flyer I have. You're the only one I can send. You have a strong mind and that's your best, your only, defence against the Waspgnat. Will you go?'

'Can I take Toots with me?' asked Olive.

'No,' replied the Wing Commander with a fierce hiss. 'You must send her home. Every minute she's here, the danger grows. I'm sure of it.'

Toots pushed her ear harder against the door. So she'd been right. The Wing Commander wanted her out of the way.

'But surely Toots is the only one who can . . .' began Olive.

'No, Brown, you don't understand them the way I do. When humans are the ones who have . . . shush, what was that?'

Toots pulled away from the door and held her breath. The wooden door had creaked beneath her ear. Had the Wing Commander heard her? She waited a moment, but no one came to the door. She looked around, then gingerly placed her ear to the wood again. Now Olive was speaking.

'Am I to go alone then?' she asked.

'Yes,' answered the Wing Commander. 'The fewer who know about this the better.'

'Ha,' thought Toots. 'The fewer people who'll be able to tell on you later, when you've got rid of the Group Captain.'

'I'd go myself,' continued the Wing Commander, 'but the Group Captain will miss me and I don't think that I would fit down the worm holes. I have to depend on you, Olive. Will you do it?'

'No, Olive, don't,' Toots begged silently.

'Yes, ma'am, I will,' replied Olive.

'Good girl. You'd better start straight away. Try not

to make any noise. If it knows you're coming it'll set a trap for you. And if it does catch you, the only shield you'll have is your mind. It's the only way to save yourself. Don't let it in. Don't let it learn why you have come, even if it tortures you, tell it nothing. I have great faith in you, Olive. I know you won't let us down. Now go, quickly, and good luck.'

Rustlings within the room warned Toots that Olive would soon be coming out. She didn't want to be caught eavesdropping so she quickly moved away from the door. She pretended to be engrossed in a map of the garden hanging on the wall, but though her eyes were glued to the map, her thoughts were full of what she'd heard.

Suspicion buzzed around her brain. It seemed so obvious to her that the Wing Commander was preparing to overthrow the Group Captain. Why else would the Waspgnat be in the garden? And as she thought this the coloured map in front of her began to fade. A shadow seeped in around the edges of her vision and Toots couldn't turn her eyes away.

'Toots! Toots!' Olive shook her and with a flash all the colours in the map returned and the lines came back into focus. 'Are you all right?' she asked. 'You're so pale.' Olive put her hand against Toots's forehead, but Toots pulled away.

'I'm fine,' she answered, but she wasn't. She felt

rattled and shaky and she didn't know why.

'You'd better go home. It's been a stressful morning. Your nerves are frayed. Let's get to the landing bay and find someone to take you.'

'Aren't you going to take me?' asked Toots.

'I can't. I have to stay here and help.'

Toots scowled. She knew why Olive couldn't take her. They didn't speak much on the way to Landing Bay Number Five.

'If you go in there,' Olive said when they arrived at the door, 'and speak to that fairy with the orange paddles, she'll get someone to take you home. I'm sorry I can't do it, but I really don't have time. Goodbye Toots, and thanks.'

Toots grabbed her arm.

'Olive, can you trust the Wing Commander?' she asked urgently. 'Don't you think she might be the one who brought the Waspgnat to the garden?'

Olive looked surprised and embarrassed at the same time. She forced a laugh. 'No, Toots, I told you, no one brought the Waspgnat to the garden. You've got it wrong about the Wing Commander. She may seem gruff, but she loves this garden. She'd never let anything happen to it, or the squadron.'

But Toots knew for certain that Olive was hiding something.

'Goodbye, Toots,' called Olive as she turned and

scuttled off down the corridor, rummaging in her bucket as she went.

Toots didn't even say goodbye. She shook her head. She didn't understand why Olive couldn't see the truth when it was so plain. Olive was acting just like her father had when he'd refused to understand why it was impossible for her to be friends with Jemma any more. Olive was refusing to see the obvious. She was refusing to see that the Wing Commander was up to no good.

But even though Toots knew Olive was making a terrible mistake, she couldn't just leave and let her go on her strange mission by herself. It was too dangerous. Olive was her friend after all, and friends were supposed to help each other, weren't they?

Toots edged away from the landing bay door and started slowly down the corridor. No one at home would miss her till later and Olive might need her help. Besides, there was a mystery here in the garden, and Toots wanted to get to the bottom of it. She ran silently along the corridor, carefully keeping so far back that Olive wouldn't suspect she was there.

CHAPTER SIX

~ The Worm Holes ~

Toots followed her friend along corridor after corridor until at last Olive stopped at a place where the painted plaster walls ended abruptly. Beyond this point lay an unlit, soil-lined tunnel which disappeared into the gloom. Olive paused by the last door in the corridor, looked around furtively, then reached into her bucket and brought out a large ball of bright blue wool and tied the end of it to the door knob. Next she took out a metal torch, flicked the switch and pointed the broad yellow beam into the dark tunnel. Transparent grains of sand sparkled in the soil and the tunnel glittered like a pavement at night. Olive followed the yellow beam into the passage, playing out the blue wool as she went.

Toots waited a moment then followed Olive. Inside the dark tunnel the air was damp and smelled richly of sodden soil and mushrooms. Whenever Olive turned a corner the light vanished with her and Toots had to run her fingers along the blue wool to make sure she was going in the right direction. She had to be careful not to pull at the wool or this might give her away.

It was warm under the earth, warm and dark and interesting. The worm holes sloped up into the ground and the higher they climbed the warmer it became.

After some time the narrow tunnel opened into a chamber with three tunnels leading off it. Olive took the tunnel on the left and halfway along this turned to her right. There were several more turns to the left then another to the right until Toots felt utterly confused. Now she understood why Olive trailed the wool behind her. Without it it would be easy to lose your way. If you got lost in this maze, you could stay lost forever, wandering round and round and never getting anywhere.

Suddenly Olive switched off her flashlight and the dark crowded in.

'Oh,' cried Toots, instantly wishing that she hadn't made any noise. She cowered in the darkness, listening as footsteps approached. There was a click and suddenly the beam of the flashlight blinded her.

'Toots!' exclaimed Olive in a whisper. 'I thought I heard something. What on earth are you doing? Why are you following me?'

'I heard what the Wing Commander told you to do and it sounded dangerous. I wanted to help. Friends should help each other, shouldn't they?'

'Yes, they should, but. . .' Olive lowered her torch and shook her head. 'Toots, you don't realize what you've got yourself into. Don't get me wrong. I'm glad for the company, this place gives me the creeps. But Toots,' Olive took her by the shoulders and looked at her very seriously, 'you must forget about everything you heard in that room. It's very important. You must clear it from your mind. Even thinking about it will put us both in terrible danger. Please, you must promise me.'

'I promise,' said Toots. 'I've forgotten it all already.'

Olive smiled at her. 'Good. But perhaps it would be best if you were to go home. If you follow the wool, you'll easily find the way back to the UDG.'

'No, I came to help you. I'm not going to back out now.'

'Very well then.' Olive fished in her bucket, brought out another torch and handed it to Toots. 'Here. But you'll have to be very quiet. And that means quiet inside your head as well as outside. That's why you must forget everything you've heard. If the Waspgnat is close by, it will be able to hear your thoughts as easily as you can hear me now. Do you understand? You mustn't go wondering off.'

Toots switched on her torch and the walls sparkled.

'Don't you mean *wandering* off?' she asked.

'Yes. But I mean don't go wondering off too. Remember, keep a good hold on your thoughts. The Waspgnat could be anywhere.'

'Where are we going?' asked Toots.

'To find the root of the problem,' was all that Olive would say.

As Toots followed Olive along the tunnels, she began to hear an unexpected sound echoing in the silence. It sounded like someone singing softly. It was a pretty melody. Toots stopped and strained her ears to try and hear better.

'Keep up,' whispered Olive, shining her light on Toots. 'You must keep up.'

'What's that singing?' Toots asked in a whisper.

Olive cocked her head to one side and pursed her lips. 'Probably someone searching for some poor soul who's lost in the worm holes.'

'Shouldn't we try and help?'

Olive shook her head sadly. 'There's no point. We'd probably never find them, not if we searched for years. That's the terrible thing about the worm holes. These tunnels distort sound. You can never tell where anyone is – that poor soul could be shouting to you from two metres away or whispering from two hundred. You'd never know.'

'If I got lost, you'd come and find me, wouldn't you?' asked Toots who was feeling a little nervous.

'You're not going to get lost. At least I hope you're not. If you did I'd never get you home in time for supper, so please keep up.'

'The singing's stopped now,' whispered Toots. 'Perhaps they've found whoever they were looking for.'

'Perhaps,' replied Olive doubtfully as she set off again.

They tramped on and on until, at long last, Olive stopped and switched off her torch.

'Turn yours off too,' she said softly.

Toots did so and to her surprise the tunnel wasn't pitch black anymore. Now it was filled with an eerie grey light like the sky just before the sun comes up.

'There must be a dog hole up ahead,' whispered Olive.

'A dog hole? Do you mean one of Binky's holes?'

Olive nodded. 'That's right. We'll have to go carefully around that.'

As they pressed on, the light became stronger, but it wasn't until they turned a sharp bend in the tunnel that they saw the large, ragged hole in the floor. Sunshine as bright as silver poured up through it and flooded into the tunnel.

Toots joined Olive at the rim of the hole and peered over the edge. She could see the broad trunk of the horse chestnut tree, its bare branches still covered in the white furzeweed seed heads. High in the branches the raven's nest swayed in the wind and beyond this the sun shone on the big white April clouds. Toots leaned forward to see better and the ground began to crumble beneath her feet. Olive pulled her back.

'Be careful,' she said. 'There's an overhang here. The earth could easily give way.'

After that Toots stayed back from the edge. She didn't want to fall into the sky. Olive stood with her hands on her hips and studied the dog hole.

'I'd fly you across, but with two of us there wouldn't be enough room and I might catch my wings on the ceiling.' She crouched down and picked up a handful of the loose soil. 'And this won't support you, it's too freshly turned, so there's no point in trying to climb around the edge.' Olive stood up, dusting the soil from her hands and gazed at the ceiling. 'I know!' she said, reaching into her bucket and pulling out her coil of cobweb rope. She flapped her wings and, taking great care not to catch them on the walls, flew up to the ceiling. Once there she began to clear away some of the soil with her hands and soon found a firm root to which she tied one end of the rope.

'Do you think you can swing across on this?' asked Olive as she landed and offered Toots the rope. Toots pulled on it. She wasn't sure. It felt sturdy enough, but what if it wasn't? What if she fell?

But Toots had promised to help and she wasn't going

to give up now. She backed up along the tunnel, wrapping the rope around her wrist. She'd done this hundreds of time in games at school, swinging on a rope across the hall, but at school there'd always been mats beneath her not the endless sky. Here there might not be any landing at all.

Toots didn't want to think of that now. She tugged on the rope, took a deep breath, then raised herself up on her toes and ran. The dog hole came up very fast and suddenly she was flying across it. The sky passed in a flash, and in less than a second she was on the other side. She let go of the rope and dropped to the ground panting with relief.

When Toots had recovered sufficiently, Olive threw the ball of wool to her, then flew carefully across the hole. She landed beside Toots, took the rope and gave it a sharp jerk. The knots around the root unfastened themselves and the rope fell down. Toots gasped.

'Could that have happened when I was swinging on it?' she asked horrified.

'Oh no,' said Olive, as she quickly coiled up the rope and dropped it back in her bucket. 'They're special fairy knots and they only come undone when I tell them to. Come on,' she said, unravelling the blue wool as she walked. 'No time to waste.'

Fifty metres further on they encountered a second dog hole. It looked as though they could cross this one in the same manner as the first and Olive was about to fix the rope to the ceiling when suddenly there was a loud 'WOOF'. Olive reacted quickly and yanked Toots out of the way just in time, for a moment later Binky's enormous brown nose shot through the hole.

Binky pushed and sniffed and snorted and sneezed and scrabbled to get as far into the tunnel as he could. He barked again and Toots thought her eardrums would explode.

'Quick,' cried Olive. 'He doesn't want to hurt us, but he could cause an accident if he's not careful.'

Olive pulled Toots back along the tunnel and they ran swiftly towards the first dog hole, but Binky was too quick for them. He sniffed them out and they heard him running along the grass beneath their feet as he scampered to the previous hole. For Toots and Olive the distance between the holes was a least fifty metres, but for Binky it was less than one metre and when they got to the first dog hole, he was already waiting for them. This time he had managed to cram his whole head into the tunnel.

'Oh you . . . dog!' said Toots as she turned to run back to the second hole. Olive caught her arm.

'There's no point,' she said. 'He'll get there before we do. We have to think of something else.' Olive stared at Binky's big wet nose. Binky scrabbled, then stopped and listened, then dug some more, then stopped again and lay there panting with his big pink tongue lolling out of his mouth. Suddenly he pushed harder and with a determined wriggle he jammed his shoulders and half his body into the tunnel. At first he was very pleased about this and Toots and Olive could hear his tail thumping on the ground outside, but when he realized that he couldn't get his head out of the hole as easily as he had pushed it in, he began to whimper piteously.

'He's stuck!' exclaimed Toots. 'He's got his big head stuck. Come on, we can get away from him now.'

'Oh no, we can't leave him like this,' said Olive, putting down the ball of wool and delving into her bucket. 'He'll suffocate.' She pulled out the cobweb rope once more and began to unfurl it. 'Come on, I'll need your help.'

'But he'll try to eat us,' cried Toots.

'No, he won't. He's just playing, just being friendly. Aren't you, boy?' said Olive. 'We have to do something to keep him quiet though, it would be better if no one knew we were here.'

Binky wailed louder. Olive pursed her lips.

'Wait here and hold this,' she said, handing Toots one end of the rope.

Binky sniffed and his nostrils widened like two wet black tunnels in the mountain of his nose. Toots could see that Olive's blue wool was caught across his muzzle.

Binky opened his jaws to try to get rid of it but the wool had tangled round his teeth. Toots could have reached out and untangled it, but instead she shrank back. Even though she knew that this was just silly old Binky, who, in the real world, didn't even reach as high as her knees, it was rather frightening to see his enormous sharp teeth up close and very unpleasant to have to smell his stinky doggy breath all around you.

'There, there, boy,' said Olive, patting Binky's nose as if his snout was a big horse. 'There you go, we'll soon have you unstuck.' Olive squeezed between Binky and the wall and tied the cobweb to the metal ring on his collar.

'Grab hold of my belt, will you?' said Olive to Toots as she backed out. 'And be prepared to take his weight.'

It wasn't until Olive said this that Toots realized what Olive meant to do. She was going to bring Binky to the Upside Down World. Toots was appalled. Binky would just be in the way. She frowned as Binky began to shrink and tutted as he whimpered louder.

'Shush boy, you'll be all right,' Olive said, looking back. 'Hold on, Toots,' she shouted. 'This could get tricky.' And she was right. When Binky had shrunk enough to be able to get himself unstuck, he pulled his head out of the hole. And he would have pulled Toots and Olive out with him, but at that moment his gravity switched. He fell upwards with his paws waggling in the air and as he fell the ball of blue wool rolled after him and dropped into the sky. There was nothing either Olive or Toots could do to stop it. All they could do was stick their heels into the ground and pull on Binky's rope with all their might.

Luckily Binky was quite small by this time. If he'd been his full size he would have dragged them out of the hole and the three of them would have been lost forever, but he was getting smaller all the time. They just had to hold on until he became small enough for them to be able to pull him inside.

'I think we can try now,' puffed Olive. 'One, two, three, heave!' Toots gritted her teeth and held onto Olive's belt and Olive gritted her teeth and held onto the cobweb rope and before long Binky appeared at the rim of the hole scrabbling frantically. As soon as he connected with the soil, he pulled himself into the tunnel and on to solid ground. Toots was relieved to see that now he was his usual size and only came up to her knees. Suddenly he bounded towards her.

'No!' she said, holding up her hands. But Binky jumped up at her anyway. He knocked her to the ground, and tried his hardest to lick her face and ears. Then he jumped back, crouched and barked once.

'Shush, shush, I know you're happy to see us,' said Olive. 'But if you're not quiet, the Waspgnat will find us and then there'll be trouble.' To Toots's amazement this had a most extraordinary effect on Binky. It was as though he understood every word that Olive said.

He stopped barking, sat down obediently and looked up at Olive with eager eyes as though waiting to hear her next command.

Olive untied the cobweb from Binky's collar and made a great fuss of him. Binky wriggled like a gleeful eel as she patted his back and scratched his ears. She untangled the remains of the blue wool which was snagged between his teeth and held up the frayed end.

'It looks like we've lost the rest of the ball,' said Olive. 'Binky must have bitten through it when he was in the air.'

'How will we find our way back now?' asked Toots who had known it was a bad idea to bring Binky to the Upside Down Garden. Olive was far too forgiving of Binky, and Toots couldn't understand why.

'Well, we know how to get back to headquarters *from* here,' said Olive nodding at the line of blue wool which disappeared into the tunnel on the far side of the first dog hole. 'But we'll need to know how to get *to* here from wherever we go. We'll have to improvise. If we make some kind of mark in the walls, something simple like this, look,' Olive dug four fingers into the soil of the right-hand wall then pulled them out leaving a perfect imprint, 'that'll show us how to get back,' she said. 'It's not as good as the wool, but it's better than nothing. Come on, let's go.'

Soon the second dog hole gaped in front of them. It seemed impossibly wide now that Binky had made it bigger. But Olive laughed.

'You've already done us a good turn, Binky,' she said, surveying the crumbled earth and the jagged hole. 'Now there's plenty of room for me to fly you both across. One at a time, of course.'

Olive picked Toots up and in an instant set her down on the far side of the hole, then she flew back for Binky, and when all three were safely on the far side, Olive made her mark in the wall and they set off once more.

As soon as they moved away from the dog holes, the worm tunnels began to lead up into the earth. Soon it grew warm and the darkness became so complete that it seemed almost to swallow up the yellow beams of their torches. Every few feet Olive dug her fingers deep into the wall and Toots, following soon after, felt the holes just to make sure that she could find the mark.

'Here, Toots, look at this,' whispered Olive as she stopped by a piece of old bottle glass embedded in the wall.

Olive rubbed the glass with her sleeve, then shone her torch through the frosted amber window. Toots pressed her face against the glass and beyond it saw acre upon acre of dark green thorns. 'Furzeweed,' she thought.

'Look how dense it grows about the roots of the tree,' said Olive, swivelling the light to the left. At first Toots couldn't even make out the huge roots of the horse chestnut tree for the thorns which were stuck into them. Then the furzeweed suddenly moved and swept towards the window in a great wave. It crashed against the glass and Toots leapt back.

'Oh, this horrible stuff,' said Olive. 'It can look so harmless and then suddenly move as though it was an animal rather than a plant.'

Olive turned to go, but something drew Toots back towards the amber window. She held her torch to the glass and shone it into the far reaches of the cavern beyond. She watched as the wave of thorns retreated and settled by the roots of the horse chestnut tree, then she directed her light on to the thicket and saw deep within the tangled thorns the same evil, grinning face she'd seen in the landing bay. Only now she could see both its yellow eyes glinting in the shadows. Its smoking mouth was open wide in a horrible grin.

As Toots stared at the mesmerizing eyes, she grew cold all over and began to hear someone laughing inside her head. It was the same horrible laugh she'd heard in the wind the night before, when the kitchen door blew open, only now the laughter was loud and strong. Toots felt suddenly angry, but she didn't know why. The reasons were all so muddled. She was angry with Jemma, with the Wing Commander, with Binky. Her head began to ache as though someone was squeezing her brain and the warm amber glow of the window started to fade. Soon, the edges of her vision became crowded with grey shadows.

'Toots?' Olive hissed, pulling Toots away from the window. The laughter stopped abruptly. Toots rubbed her eyes. The grey shadows had gone. Olive looked at her full of concern.

'You have to be strong, Toots,' Olive whispered. 'Furzeweed this active is a sure sign that the Waspgnat is close at hand. From here on we've got to be really quiet. Even quieter than we've been already. You mustn't let the Waspgnat get hold of your thoughts.'

Toots nodded and Binky growled softly as though he understood as well. Then Olive beckoned to them to follow her along the dark tunnel.

After this the tunnels grew narrower and they had to walk in single file. Olive led, Binky followed and Toots brought up the rear. The long, arduous path climbed on and on, deep into the earth.

As they travelled, Toots began to hear the strange singing again. Was it really someone searching for those who were lost in the tunnels? Toots shuddered and instinctively double checked the marks that Olive was leaving in the wall. She didn't want to get lost. The singing seemed to grow louder. Toots stopped and listened. Now she could almost hear the words. She shone her light into a tunnel on her left. It was empty, but she was sure that the singing was coming from there. Toots peered into the shadows and didn't notice that Olive and Binky were getting further away. She didn't see them disappear into the darkness.

Toots took one step closer into the empty tunnel and then another. She would have kept on walking in search of the mysterious singer, had she not remembered just in time that she was supposed to stay close to Olive. Toots turned back and ran in the direction that Olive and Binky had gone. They couldn't have walked very far in such a short time, but when she rounded the next bend, there was only darkness ahead. They were nowhere to be seen and there were no marks in the tunnel wall.

Toots ran on, desperately seeking the mark that Olive must have left. Where was it? Tears smarted in her eyes as she felt along the wall. The surface of the soil was smooth and unbroken. Suddenly it occurred to her that Olive might not have come this way, she could have turned off somewhere, could have taken a different tunnel, one that Toots, in her frantic search, had missed. Toots ran back the way she'd come, watching out for other tunnels as she went. But there weren't any others, not until she reached the one where she had heard the singing.

Panic swept over her. She knew she shouldn't scream, because she didn't want the Waspgnat to know where she was, but the need to find Olive, to call out, to yell for her, was unbearable. Whatever the consequences Toots knew that she had to find Olive. Without her she was lost. She took a deep breath, threw back her head and would have cried 'Olive!' but at that moment a hand closed over her mouth. A second hand quickly knocked her torch to the floor and the light went out as a third hand pulled her into the shadows.

CHAPTER SEVEN

~ Elizabeth ~

Toots struggled as hard as she could and tried to bite the hand across her mouth, but when a soft voice close to her ear whispered, 'Shush, please keep quiet until the wind is past,' Toots felt her fear melt away. The voice was so gentle and kind that Toots knew she'd be all right so long as she did as she was told. She stopped struggling and waited in the darkness.

The wind the voice had spoken of came quickly and as the warm air rushed up through the tunnel, the darkness seemed to change. Perhaps it was just her eyes playing tricks, but Toots was sure she could see ghostly shapes in the wind, wispy, smoky shapes that swirled swiftly through the tunnel. And each of these shapes had faint, thin, yellow eyes like slivers of lemon peel. These eyes darted here and there as though they were searching for something. Toots shrank back against the walls in case they were looking for her.

But the smoky wind quickly passed by, leaving Toots and her mysterious captor alone in the tunnel. After a moment the hands let her go. Toots immediately knelt down and, after a little fumbling, found her torch and switched it on.

She turned and was surprised to see what looked like a small, rotund old lady cowering by the wall, shading her eyes from the brilliant yellow light.

'Too bright, too bright,' whispered the old lady, waving away the torch. Toots politely pointed the beam down towards the floor, but as she did, she noticed that the old lady's hand was covered in bristly hairs, and not only that, but she had three other hands, one shading her eyes and two others pulling her tattered shawl around her shoulders. She also had two pairs of legs and these were jointed in far too many places to be mistaken for a person's legs. Toots's mouth dropped open as she realized that the old lady wasn't an old lady at all.

It was some sort of insect, she realized, no wait, it had eight limbs, and if it had eight limbs, then it was an arachnid like a spider and not an insect. Toots supposed it could be a mite. It had a long proboscis instead of a nose, stiff hairs sticking out of its hands and feet and a strange swirling pattern like that of a fingerprint all over its body.

Toots stared at all this strangeness, but didn't feel in the least bit afraid. Perhaps it was because she couldn't

quite believe what she was seeing, or because the
creature was only half as big as Toots, or maybe it was
because she could see tears caught in the hairs on the
creature's face. For whatever reason, Toots knew that
she had nothing to fear from this creature.

'What's wrong?' she asked, leaning forward.

The mite sniffed. It looked one way and then the
other, then very softly it began to sing.

> *All of my children,*
> *Poor hungry things,*
> *Lost to their mother,*
> *How my tears sting.*

> *All of my children,*
> *Poor hungry mites,*
> *Lost and so frightened,*
> *Alone in the night.*

The song resounded down the tunnels and the
echoes came back to them louder than the original
had been. This was the song Toots had heard in the
tunnels.

'So that's why you sing!' Toots exclaimed. 'You're
looking for your children. How many do you have?'

'One hundred and seventy-two,' sniffed the mite
sadly. 'You'd think that many would be easy to find, but

I can't find even one of them.'

The mite's black eyes shone with fresh tears and it dabbed at them with a small handkerchief. It was only then that Toots noticed the string muzzle that was tied so tightly around the mite's mouth and nose that it dug right into its flesh. That was why the mite could only speak in whispers. Toots winced. The muzzle looked painful.

'What's your name?' Toots asked.

'Elizabeth,' came the whispered reply.

Toots reached out and very gently tried to untie the knot, but it was too tight. The muzzle would have to be cut off.

'It's no use,' whispered Elizabeth sadly as she bent down and picked up a satchel that lay by the wall. She looped the heavy bag over her shoulder and set off at a shambling pace. After a few steps she paused and beckoned for Toots to follow. Toots looked at the mite's kind face.

'Perhaps,' she thought, 'this mite will help me find Olive.' Toots paused and shone her torch one last time in the direction that Olive and Binky had gone. The tunnel was still empty. Toots knew that if she went by herself without the marks to follow she would soon be lost and if she turned back she would only end up at the dog hole and she was sure Olive and Binky hadn't gone back there. She had to do something. Time was running out, the fairies would be leaving the garden soon. Following the mite seemed like her only option. She smiled at Elizabeth and nodded and together they set off along the tunnels.

As she followed the mite, Toots made a deep mark in the wall every five paces or so, the way that Olive had done, but Toots used only three fingers so that if Olive came to look for her, she'd know which way she'd gone.

After some time and many turns the mite stopped by a low door. She reached into her satchel, brought out a large bunch of keys, carefully selected one and slotted it into the keyhole. She gently turned the key, opened the door and slipped inside. Toots saw that the cavern beyond was crammed full of furzeweed and the thorns clacked together noisily like angry knitting needles. The mite took no notice of the noise, but, pulling a long thin knife from her bag began to hack off the tips of the nearest thorns and put them in her satchel. When she had collected ten or eleven tips she left the cavern and locked the door behind her. She slung her satchel over her shoulder, beckoned to Toots and set off once more. Now the weight of the thorns made the poor little mite list to one side as she walked.

They hadn't gone very far when the mite stopped and held up her hand.

'Turn out your light,' she hissed.

Toots did so and blinked in the sudden darkness. But

it wasn't dark for long. Soon a glow as pale as moon-light began to spread through the tunnel, making the grains of sand in the soil sparkle like stars. Elizabeth pushed Toots back against the wall.

'Keep out of sight,' she warned in a whisper.

The light grew, but it was still muted and pearly like the light inside a shell. Two strange figures appeared around a bend in the tunnel.

'Elizabeth, is that you?' demanded one of them in a high thin voice. 'Elizabeth? Come out, come out. We can hear you.'

'Eeeelizabeth,' hissed the other in a voice ever so slightly higher than the first. 'Drat the creature, sister, she should have been back with our treatment hours ago.'

'She's probably still moping about her children.'

'Her blasted children!'

'Her stinky children!'

'Her starving children.'

The two voices tittered and Toots, unable to restrain herself any longer, peeked around Elizabeth and saw two large, pudgy and blindingly white creatures coming slowly up the tunnel towards them.

They were dressed in long robes of heavy silk and on their heads they wore high crowns of multicoloured feathers and lace. Their skin was dimply and looked as soft as marshmallows and their faces were as round and as bright as big white dinner plates. They both wore small dark spectacles to hide their eyes. One creature's were made of blue glass, and the other's were red. They looked so strange, but the strangest thing of all was their skin. It was so pale and shone so brightly that it was creating the pearly light which now illuminated the whole tunnel. Toots had never seen anything like them as they glided grandly towards her, preceded by their mantle of light.

Suddenly one of them shrieked.

'Elizabeth, there you are. Where have you been?' The creature swooped down and poked Elizabeth with its dimpled finger.

'This is too, too bad,' wailed the other. 'You were supposed to be back hours ago.'

From her hiding place Toots could see how their mean little mouths pouted as they spoke. For all their grand robes they were behaving just like spoiled children.

'You know we don't like coming out into the tunnels,' whined the first.

'It's so dirty and smelly down here,' added the second with a dramatic shudder that set all her white flesh wobbling like jelly.

Toots was so fascinated by this action that she didn't notice the other creature had spotted her and so it took her by surprise when the soft doughy hand clamped firmly on to her arm.

'Sister, come quickly,' squealed the creature as she held tight to Toots.

'Ooooh! Sister, what is it?' cried the other, shoving the mite out of the way.

'Elizabeth's picked up something nasty. Just look at its foul skin. It must have come from the garden. It's all red and ruddy and burnt to a cinder by that wicked, wicked sun. I'm lucky, sister, that my skin has never suffered the effects of light.'

'Yes, and I'm lucky, sister, that mine never saw the moon, because they say, and I believe it's true, that the moon can burn you almost as badly as the sun and both are detrimental to complexions as beautiful as ours.'

They bowed their heads and smiled at each other with strained sincerity. The false smiles remained frozen on their pudgy faces. It was as though they couldn't put their faces back to normal, and this indeed was the case.

'Arghhh! Blanche,' said the one with blue spectacles through clenched teeth. 'I'm starting to dry up.'

'Oh Palydia, me too,' hissed Blanche. 'Elizabeth. ELIZABETH! Quickly, we need our treatment now. NOW! Oh, I can hardly move my mouth.' Blanche lifted both her hands to her mouth to feel if there was any sensation there and to do this she let go of Toots's wrist.

Elizabeth's eyes met Toots's. She cocked her head and tried to whisper 'Run', but Palydia saw her and gave her a sharp angry prod in the back, and Blanche recovered herself and seized Toots firmly by the ear.

'Good work, Blanche,' hissed Palydia. 'Let's take it with us. It might be useful.'

Toots squealed as Blanche dragged her along the tunnel. A hundred questions raced through her mind. Why had she been foolish enough to lose sight of Olive? Why on earth had she put her faith in a mite who wore a muzzle? And how was she going to get out of this dreadful situation? To make matters worse Blanche pulled her along so quickly that she could no longer reach the wall to make a mark. How would Olive ever find her without the marks?

The strange sisters were beginning to peel and little flakes of skin fluttered in the air as the strange procession wended its way through the dark tunnels.

CHAPTER EIGHT

~ Palydia and Blanche ~

Eventually they stopped by a door in the tunnel wall and with a grimace and a sob Palydia gingerly held out her hand. Around her wrist was a heavy silver chain and from this a small bright key dangled. Ever so gently Elizabeth took hold of the key and carefully guided it towards the keyhole in the door.

'Oww! Don't pull,' squealed Palydia. 'It hurts.' Large flakes of dried skin fluttered down from Palydia's wrist where the heavy chain chafed. 'Oww,' she groaned. 'Oh Blanche, why can't I just give her the key? Why do I have to wear it like this?'

'You know very well we can't have her running in and out of our house all the time,' replied Blanche through clenched teeth. 'You know she can't be trust-ed. She's tricky. Now shut up and move closer to the door. You're making it take forever.'

'Ow, ow, ow!' wailed Palydia as Elizabeth fitted the key into the lock. 'Turn it carefully.'

As soon as Elizabeth had turned the key, Palydia pushed past her, completely forgetting that the key was still in the door. The chain soon, brought her up sharp and Palydia screamed even louder as she ricocheted back into her sister. Blanche was not pleased.

Elizabeth gently and quickly removed the key from the keyhole, then she held the door wide open while Palydia and Blanche carefully dipped their feather crowned heads and disappeared inside. Toots didn't want to go with them, but she had no choice. Blanche's podgy white fingers still had a firm hold on her ear and where her ear went Toots had to follow.

The chamber they now entered was as different as it could be from the dark, bare tunnel. It was splendid and strange. The walls and ceilings were hung with bright silks and tall candles burned in elaborate candelabras and all this splendour was reflected in the many gold-framed mirrors on the walls. There were two carved wooden screens in the corners which displayed pictures of tiny insects and Palydia immediately disappeared behind one of these, whimpering as she went. As soon as the door was shut and locked, Blanche let go of Toots's ear and, with a muffled shriek, hurried behind the other screen.

Toots looked around. The strangest thing of all was that right in the middle of this fancy room there were two long, plain, wooden tables standing side by side.

They didn't seem to belong there at all. At the far end of one table there was a small trolley on which stood a large old-fashioned mincing machine with a huge wheel for grinding whatever was put into the funnel at the top.

Palydia soon appeared wrapped in a fluffy pink bath towel and a moment later Blanche came out in a blue one.

With a great deal of difficulty the two sisters hoisted themselves onto the tables and lay back like languishing heroines. Elizabeth gently removed their spectacles and Toots could see that all around their eyes large pieces of skin were flaking away like peeling wallpaper. It looked painful.

'Hurry!' whined Blanche without moving her mouth.

'Hurreeeee!' screeched Palydia.

Elizabeth quickly transferred the furzeweed thorns from her satchel to the mincing machine and began to turn the handle. Soon great dollops of smoothly minced furzeweed dropped into a bowl at her feet.

'Make that thing you found help you,' moaned one.

'And hurry,' groaned the other.

Elizabeth showed Toots how to turn the wheel in a continuous motion so that the minced thorn came out in one long smooth dollop. Toots turned the wheel. It was more difficult than it looked. The wheel was stiff and the furzeweed tough to grind.

While Toots struggled to turn the wheel, Elizabeth rubbed each of the sisters all over with a rough face flannel and soon the air was filled with large flakes of dried skin. Once this was done, she scooped up handfuls of minced furzeweed from the bowl and began to smear it over the sisters' rough white skin, piling it high like icing on a Christmas cake.

'Ooooh lovely, lovely,' cooed Palydia. 'I'll soon be as soft as a baby's botty.'

'Fa . . . fa . . . fa . . . fa . . . fabulous,' giggled Blanche. 'It's the most marvellous stuff for your skin. A little every day is good.'

'But lots four times a day is better!' screamed Palydia laughing. 'Thank goodness we've got enough of this stuff to last us forever and ever.'

'Thank goodness,' answered Blanche.

Toots had the hang of it now and as she steadily turned the wheel, she watched the two strange sisters get their unusual beauty treatment at the hands of the little muzzled mite. She remembered what the Group Captain had said about how the creatures who remain in a garden with a Waspgnat will behave contrary to their real nature. Ants will not work, bees will not buzz, worms will not wriggle. And she'd also said that sometimes the insects would start to talk and give themselves names and airs and graces. Toots nodded to

100

herself. That was what must have happened to these three creatures. But she was puzzled. Elizabeth was obviously a mite. But what were the two sisters? What had they been before the Waspgnat? What were they now? She stared at their strange pale skin and podgy bodies. And then suddenly she knew.

'Maggots! You're maggots!' she exclaimed.

Elizabeth looked up quickly and shook her head in warning.

'MAGGOTS?' screamed one sister sitting up sharply. 'Did you say MAGGOTS?' A dollop of green goop slid off her large face. Toots trembled.

'We're not MAGGOTS!' cried the other, wiping furzeweed sludge from her eyes. 'We are not some nasty little grubs who will turn into horrid flies. We are MaggO, MAGG-O. The T is silent. What a vile, ignorant little creature you are.'

'Now, now, you don't want to ruin the treatment and have to wait for me to go and get some more thorns, do you?' Elizabeth rested a hand on each sister's shoulder and gently guided them back down to the table. The sisters knew that Elizabeth was right, nevertheless they grumbled as they lay back down.

'We'll make you pay for that cruel remark just as soon as we've finished our treatment,' Blanche hissed.

'And we'll gag you too,' snarled Palydia. 'Elizabeth's been much better behaved since we gagged her and she hasn't eaten any more of our treatment has she, Blanche?'

'Which is quite as it should be. Imagine if we let just anyone near it. Why, there'd be none left for us. And that would be terrible.'

'Oh yes, indeed it would, sister, indeed it would.'

They lay back onto the tables and Elizabeth slathered more green goop over their faces. When the sisters were completely covered, and not one inch of their white skin was visible through the creamy furzeweed, Elizabeth turned an hourglass over and the sand began to fall.

'Why do they cover themselves in furzeweed?' whispered Toots.

'Because it's the only thing that stops them from turning into chrysalises. They don't want to do that.'

'Why not?'

'They don't want to grow up and change. Change can be a frightening thing. Terrifying! Now all they care about is their appearance. But it's not their fault,' Elizabeth's voice sank to a whisper. 'Something in the garden has made them act this way.'

Toots nodded. She knew exactly what Elizabeth meant by 'something'. She meant the Waspgnat. A frown crossed Toots's face. It was all the Wing Commander's fault and she would have told Elizabeth the whole story, but the little mite didn't seem to have time to listen. She was pushing Toots quickly towards the door.

'Hurry now,' she said urgently. 'You mustn't be here when they wake up.'

Toots tried again to untie Elizabeth's muzzle so that it wouldn't hurt her so much. 'If you have scissors, I could cut it off for you,' said Toots as she struggled with the knot.

'No,' insisted Elizabeth, casting a nervous glance at the sleeping sisters. 'There isn't time. If you are still here when they awake, they'll make you their slave, just like me. You must go.'

Toots gave the knot on the muzzle a final tug and succeeded in loosening it a little.

'Thank you,' whispered Elizabeth gratefully.

'How will we get out?'

'Blanche keeps the real key, but I have this.' And she pulled a long thin bony key from her pocket and slotted it into the keyhole. She wiggled it about, but it wouldn't turn. Elizabeth pulled it out and with a tiny file began to whittle down the points on the key. Then she tried it again. Still nothing.

'When you get out run as far from here as you can.'

'But you're coming with me, aren't you?'

Tears started in Elizabeth's eyes. 'I can't. For my children's sake, I can't.' She nodded at the two on the tables. 'They say they know where my babies are and that they'll hurt them if I try to run away.'

'How cruel,' said Toots.

The mite dabbed her eyes on her shawl. 'Oh that's not really their fault either,' she said, straightening up and trying to smile at Toots. 'It's all these strange goings on in the garden that make them that way.'

Elizabeth stopped filing and blew on the key, then she tried it in the lock again. She twisted and pulled and jiggled it, but it still wouldn't turn.

'It ought to work,' she said, throwing a worried glance at the hourglass. Time was almost up and as the last few grains of sand trickled down, Elizabeth joggled the key and gave it one enormous twist. The lock clicked open at the very moment that the sisters opened their eyes.

'Elizabeth,' they both cried sitting up. 'Elizabeth! Come and help us.'

'Go quickly,' said Elizabeth, pushing Toots out of the door with her thin hairy arms.

Toots didn't move. She was staring at the sisters. The green goop had vanished. Their skin had absorbed every drop and the difference was astonishing. The sisters glowed and their skin looked as soft and as white as summer clouds, but their eyes were red rimmed and puffy as if the light that came off their own bodies was making them smart. That was why they needed the coloured spectacles.

'Go!' said Elizabeth, pushing her through the door. Toots landed with a whumph in the dark tunnel as the door slammed shut behind her.

Remembering Elizabeth's instructions to run as far away as she could, Toots quickly jumped to her feet, switched on her torch and raced down the tunnels. She ran and ran until, believing herself incapable of running any further, she collapsed on the ground with her heart pounding in her ears.

When she was finally able to sit up she shone her torch over the smooth, dark walls, hoping to recognize something about the tunnel, but there was nothing. There were none of the marks that she or Olive had left. Toots sighed. She knew she was utterly, totally and completely lost.

She leaned back and rested her head against the wall. She was tired and hungry and was about to wonder how long it would be before she'd eat again, when she remembered the sandwiches she'd packed before she left the house. She brought them out of her pocket. They were squashed, but still edible so she quickly unwrapped one and began to nibble on a corner.

Perhaps she should have gone home when Olive insisted on it. She hadn't helped anyone. She'd only caused more trouble. Her father would be terribly worried when she didn't come home and Mrs Willets would be upset that Binky was missing. Olive had probably been looking for her for ages and would be furious with her for getting lost. Toots sat holding the half-eaten sandwich and bitterly regretted that she hadn't listened to Olive.

Then a terrible thought, a distressing nagging doubt, popped into her mind. What if Olive wasn't looking for her? What if Olive had no intention of looking for her? Toots blinked. Why would Olive not look for her, that was ridiculous? But the doubts grew. What if the Wing Commander's secret mission was more important than searching for Toots? What if Olive had abandoned her?

Toots shook her head. Olive would never do that. Olive wouldn't leave her lost and alone in the tunnels? But still the doubts crept in.

Toots thought back to when she'd last seen Olive and Binky. They had disappeared awfully quickly. Surely Olive could have turned around and seen that Toots was missing. Toots thought and thought and once again the greyness began to crowd in around the edges of her vision as the doubts raced through her mind, piling up one on top of another.

Where was Olive? Why had she let Toots get lost? Had it been part of the Wing Commander's plan all along for Olive to lose her in the tunnels? But Olive wouldn't leave her. Olive was a true friend, but then Toots had once thought that Jemma was a true friend, and she'd let her down.

The greyness crept further in and the colours in the wall opposite began to fade. Toots didn't notice. Her thoughts raced on.

Was Olive's losing her all part of the Wing Commander's plan to take over the garden? Hadn't the Wing Commander told Olive that it would be better not to have Toots around? Hadn't she wanted Olive to get rid of her?

The greyness almost filled her vision now and the doubts screamed inside her head.

Toots could see it all as clear as day. For sure, Olive wasn't her friend. Olive was a traitor. Olive was just the Wing Commander's lackey and to get some sort of promotion or reward she was willing to risk her neck and steal the Waspgnat's Olm.

A shriek of laughter echoed triumphantly down the lonely tunnel. Toots sat bolt upright filled with terror. It was the laugh she'd heard in the garden and in the tunnels and all at once she knew without a doubt that this was the Waspgnat's laugh.

Her blood grew icy cold. She knew that the Waspgnat must have heard her thoughts. She knew that it had used her to glean the information it needed. Toots hung her head. She had betrayed Olive with her thoughts. She had told the Waspgnat the purpose of Olive's secret mission. She had ruined everything.

Toots groaned. Why hadn't she heeded Olive's warning? Why had she let the Waspgnat into her thoughts? She was sure now that all those doubts she'd had about Olive had been put there by the Waspgnat. She knew that Olive wasn't a traitor. Olive wouldn't betray her or abandon her or put her in danger. But Toots had done as much for Olive and she regretted it bitterly.

The warm wind began to race through the tunnel and the air became thick with smoky grey shadows. Toots shook her head and staggered to her feet. Her legs felt like lead, but she had to get away from the awful laughter and the ghostly shapes. She switched off her torch and, still clutching the half-eaten sandwich, ran into the darkness as fast as she could, blindly feeling for any gaps in the walls which would lead her into new tunnels.

On and on she ran until her stomach ached and her legs felt as weak as straw. She ran so hard that she didn't notice that she'd left the smoky wind and the horrible laughter far behind. She kept on running until she felt her lungs would burst, then she slowed and, gasping for breath, stopped to rest in the darkness.

For a while she couldn't hear anything but the thump of her heart, but as it settled down and as she started to recover her breath, she began to hear another sound behind her in the blackness. Something else was coming quickly along the corridor towards her. It made a scrabbling, scratching, snuffling sound. Toots knew she couldn't run any more, she was too exhausted. Whatever it was, it was getting closer. Toots buried her face against her knees and held her breath, praying that it would miss her in the darkness. It didn't. Toots shrieked as it leapt on her shoulder and licked her ears, then scrabbled for the sandwich in her hand.

'WOOF!'

Toots switched on her torch and relief flooded over her.

'Binky!' she cried as the happy, wriggling dog tried to eat the sandwich and lick her face at the same time. 'You found me.'

'Woof, woof,' he yelped.

'Shush,' whispered Toots. 'Good dog! You're a clever, clever boy.'

CHAPTER NINE

~ The Tree ~

When Binky had quite finished telling Toots how pleased he was to see her and Toots had quite finished telling Binky what a smart and clever dog he was, Toots looked around hopefully. She expected to see Olive hurrying along the corridor at any moment, but no one came.

'Where's Olive?' she asked Binky, but he just wagged his tail and stood with his tongue hanging out of the side of his mouth. Toots grew worried. What had happened to Olive? It was strange that she hadn't come to find Toots. She wouldn't have gone off without her, Toots was sure of that, for all of her earlier doubts. Perhaps Olive was lost in the worm holes. Perhaps she was waiting for Toots to come and find her. Toots jumped to her feet and Binky bounced up beside her.

'Go seek,' she whispered to him. 'Come on, Binky. Go seek Olive.'

Binky seemed to understand and, with the closest

thing to a whispered woof, he put his nose to the ground and started to trace some invisible trail that only he could find. He circled twice round Toots, then set off.

'Good Boy!' Toots said chasing after him.

On they ran through the dark tunnels, but there was no sign of Olive. Toots was on the verge of despair when the beam of her flashlight struck a familiar mark in the wall. Her heart leapt. It was the imprint of Olive's four fingers. Now Toots raced ahead of Binky with her flashlight following the wall. Every few feet there was another one of Olive's imprints pointing the way. Toots hurried on. Soon everything would be all right.

But as they turned the next corner Toots's heart fell, for there in front of them was the same dog hole they had crossed before. Binky ran and stopped just short of it, then looked back over his shoulder at Toots and whimpered. Toots crouched down beside him and stroked him gently. Binky hadn't brought her to Olive, he had brought her home, or as near to home as he could bring her. She couldn't be angry with him about that. But this didn't help matters much. She still had to find Olive, and they still had to save the garden.

Toots sighed as she realized that she'd been following Olive's marks in the wrong direction and that was why they'd led her back to the dog hole. But suddenly she sat up. They couldn't be the same marks. If they were, they would have been in the left wall and these were in the right. Olive must have come back this way. Perhaps she'd been looking for Toots. Toots stood up and shone her light over to the other side of the dog hole. There was a fresh mark in the far wall. Olive must have returned to headquarters, probably to form a search party to look for her.

Toots was sure of it. She smiled and shone her light into the shadows far beyond the sunlit hole to see if she could see any sign of her friend. Something glinted on the ground. Toots couldn't quite make out what it was so she stood up and held her light a little higher. Then she saw that Olive's torch lay abandoned on the ground and all around it the soil had been churned up and there were kick marks in the wall. It looked as though there'd been a fight. Toots frowned.

'Something terrible must have happened to Olive,' she thought. 'Perhaps she was captured by the Waspgnat.'

If that was the case, there was only one course of action open to her. She would have to do for Olive what she supposed Olive had been trying to do for her. She would have to go back to headquarters and get help. It didn't matter if the Wing Commander bellowed at her, she had to help Olive.

Toots studied the wide hole in front of her. How was

she going to get across? There was no ledge around it and the dirt was too loose to provide any footholds. And even supposing she made it, how would Binky get across?

Toots looked around and noticed a twisted root embedded in the wall. She stretched over as far as she dared and gently scraped the dirt away. When she had removed as much soil as she could, she slotted her fingers beneath the root and pulled. It unravelled easily from the wall.

The root was old and brown. It seemed strong, but would it be strong enough to carry her weight to the other side? Holding it in both hands she pulled with all her might. Behind her Binky latched on to it with his teeth and pulled as well. The root held.

'It'll do,' Toots declared.

Even though Olive was missing, Toots was beginning to feel a little better about the whole situation. At least now she knew where she was. All she had to do was get across the two dog holes, then follow the blue wool back to headquarters and form a rescue party. She was sure that with the help of the other fairies she'd soon be able to find Olive. For the first time Toots felt that she was getting somewhere. Now if she could just get across the dog holes, everything would be all right.

She lifted Binky and held him under one arm, then she clutched the root with her free hand, and, on the count of three, launched herself over the edge.

In less than a moment her feet were touching the far side of the hole. In a flash Binky wriggled out of her grasp, scrambled over her and leapt onto the edge. At first Toots thought he was just trying to save himself and was a little annoyed, but then she realized that once he was out of the way it was much easier for her to pull herself up. She paused for a moment clinging to the root while her feet sought a firm foothold on the edge. Just then a dark shadow passed over her and a loud screech shattered the silence.

'KRONK!'

It was so loud that Toots lost her footing and swung out over the hole. She looked down and saw an enormous raven staring at the waggling root with an unmistakable gleam of intent in his bright eye.

'Oh no, he thinks it's a worm,' thought Toots as she struggled to swing back towards the ledge. But before she could even touch the other side with her feet, the raven had grabbed the root in his beak and was pulling on it ferociously.

'Let go,' Toots screamed. 'Go away!' But the raven, not being her way up, couldn't hear her and continued to pull. The root groaned and creaked.

'No,' cried Toots, knowing that if it gave way she would fall into the sky and be lost forever.

But the raven continued to pull and suddenly, with a

great crack, the root split. Toots screamed as she fell towards the clouds.

Binky barked after her.

'Kronk!' cawed the raven, finding he'd caught nothing but a dry dead root.

Toots's fall was fast and surprisingly short. Before she'd even had time to realize that she was falling, it was over. It was lucky for her that the raven's messy nest at the top of the tree lay directly in her path. Toots crashed right into the bottom of it and lay there breathless staring up at the garden.

She ran her hand through the deep layer of white feathery seed heads that covered the underside of the raven's nest. Most of them had their tiny white seeds attached. Now that the fairies were leaving the garden. Toots could tell that the furzeweed would soon take over.

Toots gazed up at the tree's thick trunk and sprawling roots and sighed. Now she was even further away from finding Olive. It was so frustrating. Toots shook herself. There wasn't much time. She had to get to the fairies before they left the garden for good. She'd never be able to find Olive by herself and without Olive how would she ever get back to her own world? Time was running out for the horse chestnut tree as well, she thought sadly. Mr Phelps had promised to come round at four o'clock that afternoon and it must be after lunch time already. There had to be something she could do, there had to be some way to defeat the Waspgnat, some way to save the garden and the tree, some way to find her friend, but lying there thinking about it wasn't going to help.

Toots squinted up at the enormous tree. Perhaps if she climbed up to the roots, she could find a way back into the Upside Down Garden. Slowly she got to her feet and, remembering how her father always said that 'even the longest journey starts with a single step', she set off walking carefully along the underside of a thick branch, kicking through the seed heads.

In a little while she came to a branch which climbed steeply towards the trunk. Toots scurried up it on all fours and soon reached the top.

She had expected that climbing the tall trunk would be the most difficult part of the journey, but she was wrong. She soon found that there were large crevasses behind the bark and she could actually climb inside these which made it much safer. It was like climbing up an old worn staircase with a banister of bark to keep her from falling. Now Toots made great progress as she concentrated on climbing step by step, counting each one as she went.

She had just reached seven hundred when she heard someone crying. The noise came from inside a knothole in the wood. Cautiously, Toots shone her torch through the hole. Behind the bark was a large cavern and it was crammed full of tiny baby mites who were all sniffling and weeping quietly to themselves. Toots put her hand over the end of her torch to soften the light.

'These are Elizabeth's children!' she thought. 'Poor little things.'

The mite closest to her tried to raise its head, but it didn't have the strength. Toots knelt down beside it.

'What's the matter?' she whispered.

'We're hungry,' it whimpered.

'So hungry,' rasped another one.

'Please help us,' begged a third.

'Don't worry,' said Toots. 'I'll get help.'

A murmur ran through the cavern of the poor mites.

'Hurry, hurry, please hurry,' they wheezed in unison.

'I will, I promise.'

Toots squeezed back through the hole and continued her steady climb up the tree. She focused her mind and concentrated on each step and she soon reached the bottom of the tree. A little way off, between two of the roots, she could see a dark hole and beside it was the scar in the shape of the number three. Toots knew that this was the entrance to Landing Bay Number Three, but as she rested in the bark and stared at the entrance she could not for the life of her work out how to get to it.

CHAPTER TEN

~ The Roots ~

Getting to the entrance was going to be difficult. Unlike the tree trunk the roots were smooth and bare and there were no deep crevasses that would provide easy footholds.

Toots stared up at the smooth roots. It was horrible being able to see just where you wanted to go and not being able to think of a single way to get there. She concentrated as hard as she could and all at once remembered what her father always told her to do whenever she was stuck with her homework. 'Try and look at the problem from another angle,' was his advice. 'Look at it another way.'

Toots twisted her head down and looked at the roots, but it was no use. There were still no handholds . . . unless . . . she dipped her head a little farther over. Then she saw it. Just where the root connected with the ground it looked as though there was a ledge. Toots stood on tiptoe and reached up with her hand to feel. It was a ledge, a little lip and it was just big enough for her hands to fit inside. She might be able to hang onto it and inch her way along to the hole. It wasn't going to be easy, but she didn't have a choice. Everything depended on her getting to that entrance. Everything. With both hands she grabbed hold of the ledge and swung out on to the root.

It was hard to hold on because the root bowed out towards her like a big belly, but Toots took a deep breath, slipped her left hand along the ledge, then slid her right up to meet it. In this way she advanced slowly, concentrating only on the movement of her hands.

Her fingers ached and she wished she could move faster, but she knew speeding up could be fatal. It was better to go slowly. She soldiered on until, at last, she was hanging right over the entrance. Now all she had to do was swing her legs just a little to the right and drop down. She didn't want to give herself time to get scared, so she swung her legs, quickly counted to three and let go.

She landed just inside the tunnel and gasped with relief. She'd made it! But when she rolled over and looked into the shadows between the roots, her heart sank. It was crammed tight with sharp furzeweed thorns. She looked back up at the root. There was no way she could reach it. She was trapped in the entrance.

It was all the Wing Commander's fault, she thought angrily. If it hadn't have been for her and her stupid ambitions, none of this would have happened. None of it. Olive would be all right, the tree wouldn't be about to be cut down and the garden wouldn't be dying. If it wasn't for the Wing Commander there wouldn't be a Waspgnat. Toots was sure of that. Her anger welled inside her and with it came a torrent of other grievances. Ugly memories popped into her head un- invited. She remembered how the Wing Commander had been so rude to her, and how Olive had been told to send her home. How she'd been ordered to get her out of the way. Toots seethed as she thought about the Wing Commander's treachery and in the same moment she remembered how angry she'd been with Jemma for breaking her promise. Now that anger felt ten times as sharp and painful as it had on the day Jemma let her down. It boiled in her brain and once more her vision became tinged with grey shadows and Toots fumed. She would never ever be friends with Jemma again.

Suddenly the Waspgnat's laugh shrieked all around her. It was louder than she'd ever heard it before. Toots clamped her hands over her ears, but she couldn't blot out the awful sound. She looked for some way to escape, but she was trapped. There was nowhere to run.

Just then the furzeweed at the entrance untangled

itself and a large gap appeared in the thorns. Through it Toots could vaguely make out the row of landing lights in the distance. It was the landing bay.

She hesitated. Even though she wanted to get away from the Waspgnat's wild laughter, she knew that if the thorns could move apart they could just as easily move together. What if she ran into the tunnel and the thorns squeezed her to death? Behind her the horrible laughter screamed even louder and suddenly Toots didn't care what happened in the tunnel. She just had to escape from that noise.

The moment she ran through the hole in the thorns the Waspgnat's laughter stopped. Toots was relieved and took her hands away from her ears, but an instant later there was a loud whirring clatter as the thorns snapped shut behind her, sealing off her exit.

Toots advanced, keeping her eyes on the dim lights in the distance and carefully avoiding the sharp thorns which clacked menacingly as she passed.

When she reached the cavernous landing bay she saw that it, too, was crowded with thorns. She stepped carefully on to what had once been the fairies' runway and, remembering that if she followed the long line of lights it would lead her to the doors, she set off.

Toots hurried, but when she got to where the doors should have been she could see that there was no way through. Here the furzeweed grew thick, crowding around the metal doors like iron filings around a magnet. Toots tried to pull the thorns away, but they wouldn't budge.

'Oh!' she cried, hitting the furzeweed angrily with her fists. Tears welled up in her eyes. But before one tear spilled onto her cheeks the Waspgnat's laughter rose again like a shrill wind and this time a hundred raw voices joined with it and began to screech like birds.

Toots covered her ears. The Waspgnat laughed louder. She pressed her hands harder against her ears, expecting the noise to go on forever, but just as suddenly as before, it stopped.

The silence was shocking. Toots gazed around her. The landing lights were growing dimmer. Or were they? No. They were just as bright as they had been, but they were beginning to lose their colour as though someone had thrown a grey veil over them. Toots blinked. She'd felt like this before when she'd been angry in the worm holes and at the entrance to the landing bay, but now the feeling was stronger and the colours were fading fast. Within moments everything was coloured black and white and shades of grey, like an old film she'd once seen.

'What are you doing to my eyes?' she cried.

Her only answer came in a short burst of the bird-like chatter. A warm wind started to blow and

Toots grew frightened as the greyness in front of her began to break up into hazy shapes which danced through the air like wisps of grey silk. They were the same shapes she had seen in the wind in the tunnels. She could see their pale lemony eyes.

The bird-like chatter began again. It was louder this time. Toots wanted to cover her ears, but a thick band of grey smoke wrapped itself around her body and she couldn't even lift her hands away from her sides. She tried to struggle and cry out, but it was no use. A long wispy strand covered her mouth and a thick bandage of black smoke enveloped her eyes. As the twin lines of grey runway lights vanished, the Waspgnat's laughter rose menacingly in the gloom.

Many smoky hands lifted Toots up. All around her the thorns clattered and the bird-like voices shrieked, and above it all the Waspgnat laughed and laughed and laughed.

CHAPTER ELEVEN

~ The Waspgnat's Lair ~

How far they carried her or for how long, Toots didn't know, but eventually she was set gently on the ground and the laughter and the bird-like screams and the clacking of the thorns stopped. The blackness in front of her eyes dissolved to grey and Toots found that she could move freely.

She looked around and saw that she was in a huge empty dome-like chamber. The walls, the floor and the ceiling were covered with tightly woven furzeweed. There were no doors or windows, but a thin yellow light shone through the interlaced thorns and threw criss-cross shadows over the floor. It was a treacherous light.

Toots was scared right down to her bones. What was this terrible place? Cautiously she moved around the edges of the room trying to find a way out. She touched the wall, and the cavern shook with a thunderous din. The interwoven furzeweed contracted and the light faded as the thorns drew closer together.

Toots leapt away from the wall and tripped as her foot caught between the thorns on the floor. Something beneath the thorns grabbed hold of her foot. She tried to pull away, but whatever it was held on fast.

'Toots! Toots!' hissed a familiar voice. Toots stopped struggling and held still. 'Toots, it's me, Olive!'

Toots peered down between the thorns in the floor and saw Olive's pale face staring up at her.

'Olive!' whispered Toots. 'Are you all right?'

'The Waspgnat caught me. It knew why I had come,' she whispered. Toots felt awful. That was all her fault. But Olive didn't give her a chance to explain. 'It's been trying to make me into a wraith,' she continued, 'but it hasn't managed it yet. I guess I'm a tough nut to crack.' Olive smiled weakly. Toots could tell that she was exhausted.

'Olive, don't worry, I'll get you out of here.'

'Be careful, Toots,' whispered Olive. 'Be careful. And keep moving. I think its wraiths can only get a good hold of you if you stand still.'

'Olive, don't worry,' whispered Toots. 'I'll get you out of here. There has to be a way. There has to be!'

All at once the yellow light grew brighter.

'Oh, but there is, my dear,' murmured a laughing voice. And though it was now as sweet and melodic as

Christmas bells, Toots felt her heart grow cold.

'Indeed there is,' the Waspgnat continued. 'And such an easy way, such an easy way.' Then the voice vanished like smoke in the wind. Toots spun around. She could see no one.

'Toots, be careful,' hissed Olive. 'Guard your mind, you know it can read your thoughts.'

Toots looked down. Grey forms were wrapping themselves about her body. She had stayed still for too long.

The Waspgnat laughed again and the thorns rippled all around the walls like waves on the ocean.

'What do you want?' Toots cried.

Her voice echoed around the empty cavern and bounced back ten times louder than before.

'WHAT DO YOU WANT?' it bellowed. The sound was so distorted and loud that she barely recognized her own voice.

'Stop it!' she cried again. But the echo shouted back at her 'STOP IT . . . STOP IT . . . STOP IT . . .' and the Waspgnat's laughter shrieked above it.

'Oh dear, poor Toots, poor Toots,' the Waspgnat whispered in a sing-songy way which made Toots's skin crawl. 'Let's get a better look at you.'

Above her, the thorns in the dome clacked angrily. Toots could hardly move her head, it felt as though her neck had seized up. With a huge effort she turned her face towards the ceiling. The thorns were unravelling from the centre of the dome and falling back towards the ground. The yellow light was growing stronger. It almost blinded Toots, but she could not look away.

The thorns unlaced themselves quickly and settled in a thick bank around the edges of the cavern. Toots stared up and as her eyes grew accustomed to the light she could see that something large and sinister was sprawled across the ceiling. She shuddered.

It was the Waspgnat.

The Waspgnat was gnarled and ancient, like a strange kind of mangled root vegetable that has been left to rot. Countless limbs lay in a jumble, crossing and criss-crossing each other like so many mouldy parsnips with long stringy ends. A thin wisp of black smoke curled around the tip of each root-like limb and each wisp coiled into the air, then danced away and faded amongst the grey shapes.

For a moment Toots felt relieved. The horrible grey shapes were nothing but a little smoke.

The soft voice laughed again. 'Oh no, not just smoke, my dear. Oh no, no, no, not just smoke, not smoke at all. These are my little friends, my children, my workers. These are my wraiths and they've been so looking forward to meeting you.'

The Waspgnat lifted its limbs and little puffs of smoke shot out and swirled through the air. Toots could now see faces forming in the grey smoke, faces with narrow, yellow eyes and sharp, mean little mouths. The wraiths opened their mouths and chattered like birds at dawn.

Toots watched mesmerised as they danced through the air. They twirled and somersaulted and flew right up to the ceiling, twisting in and out of the tangled thorns.

'Wouldn't you like to play with my pretties?' asked the Waspgnat in its soft, insinuating voice. 'Doesn't it look like fun to do just what they're doing?'

Toots laughed as one shadowy creature brushed agained her. It was warm and soft and it tickled her.

'See, it's fun, isn't it?' said the Waspgnat. 'Now wouldn't you like to fly? Wouldn't that be nice? Why don't you give it a go?'

The thin grey shadows twirled themselves around Toots's arms and tightened. Yellow eyes gazed up at her. The mean little mouths smiled. Toots felt a slight pressure on her arms, then suddenly she was lifted off the ground.

Toots laughed. She couldn't help it. It felt as though she was floating through the air. When she'd flown with Olive, she'd had to hold on so tight that it hadn't been very comfortable, but this was wonderful. She felt so light. The wraiths on either side of her swooped like swallows, guiding Toots over the bank of thorns and up towards the Waspgnat where it smouldered on the ceiling.

'That's right, my pretties, bring her close to me, bring her up and let me have a nice long look at her,' cooed the Waspgnat.

Toots grew a little nervous as she flew towards the sprawling, tangled mass.

She could see faces in the wrinkles and crevasses of the roots. She no longer liked flying. She didn't want to get so close to the strange root on the ceiling. Toots knew that she was in the wrong place. The faces she could see were evil and cold. She wanted to struggle against the soft hold of the wraiths, but the smoke which curled about her arms was deceptively strong. The narrow yellow eyes mocked her and the laughter began again.

'Oh dear,' laughed the soft voice. 'You wanted to come up here, but now you want to run away. This will never do.'

And as it said this the lumpy bulbous centre of the root rolled back and two long, narrow, yellow eyes with jet black pupils as cold as fish unlidded themselves in the pulpy, ochre flesh. A thin wide slit of a mouth opened like a knife wound.

It was the face Toots had seen hiding in the thorns, only now it was so much bigger and so much more terrifying.

The mouth slit grinned and bared two rows of tiny yellow teeth. Wisps of grey smoke curled in and out of the cavernous mouth and looped around the charcoal-black tongue which lolled behind the teeth.

'What's the matter, my dear?' asked the soft voice with a mocking tone which had not been there before. 'You seem a little taken aback. Surely you're not afraid of me?'

Toots couldn't answer, for though she could see the mouth moving and hear the words, she knew that the soft voice didn't belong in that wide ugly mouth. The Waspgnat laughed and shifted its position on the ceiling. As it moved, Toots glimpsed the large purple rock that lay embedded in its chest.

'The Olm!' she thought, but as soon as the thought entered her head, she regretted it. The Waspgnat laughed and smoke poured out of its mouth.

'Oh yes, I know why you're here. Don't you remember you told me?' it snickered. 'You came here to steal my jewel, my power, my precious Olm. Just like that other one. Ha!'

The Waspgnat laughed again and Toots almost choked on the clouds of billowing smoke. The wraiths laughed too, high and shrill like a hundred hungry starlings clamouring for food.

Toots coughed and spluttered and her eyes smarted from the smoke. She had to get away from this vile and poisonous thing, but she couldn't move against the wraith's firm grasp.

'You can't leave so soon.' The Waspgnat's voice broke a little now. Roughened by the smoke, it had lost its softness and now had a menacing edge. 'I'd like to keep you with me, always. See how well I treat my guests. I turn them into happy little wraiths. You'll fit in so well.'

'No,' cried Toots, but two wisps of smoke formed themselves into claw-like hands. They grabbed her face and squeezed her cheeks together until her lips puckered.

'You know that I don't come here uninvited.' The Waspgnat shrieked with laughter. 'Who do you think brought me to the garden?'

Toots was startled. Did this mean that the old stories were true? Had she been right all along?

The Waspgnat laughed even harder. 'Who do you think brought me here?'

Toots didn't want to think about who'd brought the Waspgnat to the garden. She didn't want to think about anything at all.

But the smoky claws held her head and Toots found herself staring deep into those evil yellow eyes with their fathomless black pupils.

It was terrible to feel those awful eyes on hers. It felt as though the Waspgnat could see every bad or unkind thought she'd ever had. Toots tried to look away and close her eyes, but she couldn't. The wraiths had her in their grasp and there was nothing she could do to get away from the Waspgnat. She squirmed as those eyes bored deep into her soul. The nasty wide mouth with its black tongue and rows of tiny teeth smiled in an ever widening grin. It seemed to grow so big that in one gulp it could swallow her whole and for a moment Toots thought that this was what it was going to do.

The Waspgnat laughed and smoke wafted out between its teeth. 'Oh dear me, no, child, I don't want to eat you. I want to help you.'

Toots felt like screaming that she didn't want the kind of help that the Waspgnat had to offer, whatever it was, but she couldn't open her mouth to speak. She couldn't even hold on to her own thoughts because the Waspgnat was rapidly gaining control of them.

Now, Toots couldn't hear anything but the Waspgnat's voice, couldn't see anything but the Waspgnat's eyes, couldn't feel anything but smoky hands holding her head, could hardly think of anything but the Waspgnat. And then one by one the thoughts popped into her mind as clear as day. How right she'd been to criticize the Group Captain because she was so small, how sensible it was of her to mistrust Olive because she had abandoned her, and how brilliant of her to know that the Wing Commander was up to no good and wanted to take over the garden for herself. The Waspgnat smiled broadly and Toots smiled back at it.

'Now are you ready to give me your whole mind?' croaked the Waspgnat.

Toots gazed deep into the black eyes and saw nothing but comfort and joy and satisfaction couched within those shadowy depths.

'Yes,' she replied in a dreamy voice.

'Good. Now I will blow on your weaknesses, and kindle those flames of fear. Whatever it is that makes you weak, I will encourage in your heart and soon you will be consumed and destroyed by it. I see your anger and fear, your mistrust and suspicion. Now I can see everything.'

The Waspgnat's eyes rolled back until the black pupils disappeared completely, leaving two empty yellow slits. Thin wisps of snow-white smoke coiled out of the corners of its eyes and snaked through the air towards Toots. The Waspgnat laughed and laughed and more smoke billowed out of its mouth as though it would never stop.

The coils of white smoke came closer and closer. Toots could do nothing to stop them, they were almost touching her face when suddenly an ear-splitting howl tore through the room.

'WHAOOOOO WOOO WOOO WOOO!'

The Waspgnat and the wraiths stopped laughing

and the white smoke curled back like a thief's fingers caught in the act.

Only Toots wasn't disturbed by the strange howl. She smiled as though the noise was nothing, but a sweet distant dream. Sleepily she stared down into the cavern and saw Binky. He threw back his head and wailed.

'WHAOOOOO WHAOOOO!'

'Binky,' she thought through the haze of smoke in her mind. Behind Binky she could see the hole he had dug through the furzeweed. He had dug his way in to come and find her. At his feet there was another hole and Olive was already climbing out through it.

'Arghh!' screamed the Waspgnat with smoke flying out of its mouth. 'Look what it's done to my beautiful furzeweed! Get that animal. Get it!'

All but two of the wraiths that held Toots tight, raced down towards Binky and Olive. Binky howled again and Olive quickly unlooped her coil of cobweb rope and twirled it above her head like a lasso.

Wraiths circled Olive trying to get a hold on her, but she was too quick and strong for them. She wafted them away. Binky barked and ran around in circles and wriggled furiously so that the wraiths couldn't get hold of him.

'Don't worry, Toots, I'll get you down,' Olive cried. 'Don't give in to it. Whatever you do, don't give in to it.'

'Look at me, little girl,' insisted the Waspgnat. 'Look at me.'

Against her will, Toots turned back to face the creature on the ceiling. The yellow eyes were now as bright as flames and the thin wisps of snow-white smoke coiled towards her once more. Toots screwed up her face, but she couldn't close her eyes.

'You're going to be mine, little girl,' hissed the Waspgnat. 'You're going to stay here with me.'

Toots tried to say no, tried to shout, to scream, but she couldn't make any noise. She could only stare into those terrifying yellow eyes and nod.

But suddenly Olive's lasso looped over her foot and she felt a tug at her ankle. As the white smoke coiled towards her, Toots dropped several feet towards the floor and the white smoke clutched at nothing. The wraiths holding Toots's arms tried to pull her back up. They scowled and set their mean mouths in foul grimaces. Olive tugged again and though the wraiths pulled back, Olive was the stronger and Toots dropped all the way to the floor.

As soon as Toots was on the ground, Olive grabbed her. 'Don't look back! Come on, we don't have much time. The furzeweed will work out how to mend itself and close the hole soon enough. Let's go.' Olive pushed Toots towards Binky's hole. All around them the furzeweed shuddered and clacked, trying to bring its sharp thorns across the hole. But, for the moment, it couldn't seal the gap. Binky shot through the hole and Toots hurried after him, but just as she was about to escape, the Waspgnat screamed.

'AWAY, WRAITHS! LET ME HAVE THEM!' In an instant the smoky wraiths vanished.

Toots looked up at the ceiling and froze.

'Go!' cried Olive, but Toots couldn't move.

'It's coming down,' she whispered. Olive looked up. Toots was right.

The Waspgnat writhed furiously Each rootish limb bristled and buckled and detached itself from the ceiling, and the Waspgnat started to move. It came down quickly, scuttling like a spider. Hunchbacked and foul, its gnarled limbs scurried down the walls and over the ground with an evil lopsided gait. Its roots wriggled and crawled over each other. Smoke streamed from its mouth, from its eyes and from the ends of its roots, and in the shadows behind it a host of yellow-eyed wraiths waited.

'Look!' cried Toots as the Waspgnat charged towards them. Embedded deep in its chest was a purple rock. The Olm. Toots knew what she had to do. If she could only smash that rock. If she could only destroy the Olm. Everything would be all right. It was so close. There had to be something she could do!

'I can hear your thoughts, little girl. I know what you

want. Come and try to get it. Ha ha ha!' laughed the Waspgnat.

'Toots, no. There isn't time!' Olive insisted. 'It will destroy you.'

But Toots didn't hear her. Quickly she hunted in Olive's bucket. There had to be something in there that would do the trick. She found a hammer and took it out.

As the Waspgnat thundered towards them, Toots stood up, hammer in hand, ready to face it.

'No, Toots!' yelled Olive, grabbing her arm and dragging her into the tunnel.

'I have to!' cried Toots, but Olive pulled her harder. Behind them the Waspgnat shrieked with laughter.

'Most of this garden is mine already! Now I'm going to get the rest.'

Toots, Olive and Binky fled into the darkness while all around them the thorns clacked and the wraiths screeched.

CHAPTER TWELVE

~ Back to Headquarters ~

Binky ran on ahead down the narrow tunnel he'd dug through the furzeweed. Toots followed, then Olive. It was difficult for Olive because of her size and she had to wriggle and crawl as fast as she could. All the time the furzeweed clacked and the wraiths shrieked behind them.

When Toots finally emerged breathless at the other end Binky was waiting for her. He barked joyfully and licked her face and ears as she came out of the hole. Toots didn't have the strength to push him away.

'The Waspgnat will be after us soon enough,' warned Olive as she wriggled out of the hole. 'That wasn't an idle threat that the Waspnat made about its final attack. We've got to get back to Headquarters as fast as we can.' But before they left they quickly blocked up the hole with soil. 'It's not much,' said Olive patting down the dirt. 'But it might keep the furzeweed at bay for a little while.'

'Olive, why did you stop me from taking the Olm?' asked Toots in frustration. 'I could have smashed it. I could!'

'No. If you'd gone back then, the Waspgnat would have destroyed you,' said Olive firmly. Toots knew she was right and didn't say any more.

Olive took Toots's torch and switched it on. They were back in the worm holes. The dark walls sparkled and there on the ground lay Olive's original trail of blue wool. At least this meant that they were on the fairy headquarters side of the dog holes. Toots looked at Olive and waited for her to say which way they should go. Olive bit her lip and shone her light first in one direction and then the other. She shook her head. There was nothing to show her which way would lead them back to headquarters and which would take them on to the dog holes.

Olive shone the light on a large dark stain that was growing on the wall.

'The furzeweed is breaking through,' she cried. 'Whichever way it is we've got to hurry.' Olive set off in one direction, but Binky put his nose to the ground, barked and set off at a run in the other. Olive turned around.

'Good dog,' cried Olive. 'Quick, come on, Toots. He knows the way.'

The stain on the wall began to buckle and suddenly

a huge furzeweed thorn shot out into the tunnel. Toots screamed and set off at a run after Olive and Binky.

Far behind them they could hear the screams of the wraiths and the clack-clack of the furzeweed's thorns. Toots tried not to listen. On and on they ran, never pausing to catch their breath.

As Toots ran in the darkness, her thoughts ran on in her head. She couldn't stop thinking about how the Waspgnat had asked her over and over again, 'Who do you think brought me to the garden, eh? Who do you think invited me in?' Toots knew for certain that it was all the Wing Commander's doing, but if she was so sure, why did the Waspgnat's question make her so uneasy?

Toots was so lost in thought she didn't notice that Olive had stopped and she ran right into the back of her.

'Quiet,' said Olive switching off her torch.

A little way ahead the tunnel glowed with an eerie white light and above the noise of the wraiths and the furzeweed, they could hear something wailing.

'What is it?' whispered Toots.

'I'm not sure,' replied Olive.

They crept forward. The light grew brighter and the wailing more distinct. Binky slunk ahead of them and with his head low and his ears flat he vanished around the next corner.

Moments later they heard him howl so piteously that Toots cried out, 'Binky!' and hurried after him.

She didn't have to go far. She found Binky around the next corner and soon saw what had made him howl.

The Maggot sisters, Blanche and Palydia, were slowly making their way down the tunnel. They were in a terrible state. Their drying skin was flaking off, their fine clothes were in tatters, they had lost their feather crowns and their spectacles and their eyes were red and raw from crying. Blanche was struggling with a bulging suitcase, while Palydia carried the heavy mincing machine in a basket. In front of them their furniture moved slowly forward in a dangerously high and swaying stack.

'Why do we have to leave our lovely home?' wailed Blanche through her almost dried-up lips.

'Can't we just stay?' sobbed Palydia crying even louder.

'Hey,' cried Toots as she and Olive hurried up to them.

'Oh!' cried the sisters shying away from her. 'Don't hurt us!'

'Where's Elizabeth?' asked Toots. 'What have you done with her?'

'Oh,' wailed Palydia. 'That dreadful stuff invaded our home.'

'Nasty sharp thorns,' cried Blanche.

'Our lovely home all gone, all gone,' wailed Palydia.

'Toots, we've got to hurry,' urged Olive. Binky barked. The screeching wraiths were getting closer and more dark stains were growing on the walls. The furze-weed would soon catch up with them if they didn't keep moving.

'What have you done with Elizabeth?' Toots demanded. Blanche nodded weakly at the huge stack of furniture and Toots peered at it. It took her a moment to realize that Elizabeth's small brown face was poking out from beneath all the chairs and tables and mirrors and folded curtains. The little mite was carrying the whole lot on her back.

'Oh poor Elizabeth,' said Toots, pushing past the Maggot sisters. 'How cruel. Quick, Olive, have you got any scissors?' Olive reached in her bucket and pulled out a pair.

'She insisted on carrying it all,' reasoned Blanche, dropping her basket.

'Yes, it was all her idea,' insisted Palydia, sitting down with a flump on her suitcase.

Toots ignored them and, hurrying to Elizabeth, quickly cut through the ropes that tied the furniture to the mite's back. With a great heave she pushed the chairs and tables and curtains to the floor. The mirrors smashed against the wall. Then Toots gently snipped through the muzzle that was tied so tightly around

Elizabeth's mouth.

'Thank you,' said Elizabeth, opening her mouth wide with relief.

'Toots,' cried Olive. 'Let's go.' Olive was right, the furzeweed was not far behind them now and the warm wind of the wraiths had begun to blow through the tunnel.

'Oh!' wailed Blanche and Palydia. Elizabeth rushed back to them.

'They'll be in terrible danger if we leave them here,' she cried as she helped Blanche to her feet.

'But they were so horrible to you,' cried Toots. 'Why do you want to help them?'

'I can't just leave them,' replied Elizabeth.

'Elizabeth's right, Toots,' said Olive. 'We have to take them with us. But they can't bring their baggage. We'll move much faster without it.'

Olive put an arm around Palydia and half carried her, and Elizabeth and Toots supported the wailing Blanche while Binky ran ahead to lead the way through the dark tunnel.

With Binky's smart nose and the blue wool to guide them they soon came to the end of the worm holes and found themselves in the deserted corridors of fairy headquarters. Their quick footsteps rang out along the neatly tiled floor.

It looked as though the corridor had been

abandoned in a hurry. Doors were half open, lights were left on and half-packed baskets lay haphazardly in the corridor. Olive pushed them out of the way as they hurried past.

They hadn't got very far along the corridor when there was a great clatter of thorns behind them. Toots looked back. The entrance to the worm hole was now completely blocked with thorns and more were sprouting up by the second. Cracks raced along the green painted walls, splitting the plaster as the thorns fought their way through. Toots and Elizabeth ran faster, half pulling, half carrying Palydia between them.

'Come on,' cried Olive over her shoulder. 'This way.'

She turned down a corridor on the left and at the far end of it Toots could see the large metal doors and the sign which said 'Landing Bay Number One'. They all raced towards it.

With terrifying speed the furzeweed broke through the walls and the ceiling. Toots could hear the horrible chatter of the wraiths and somewhere far behind this she could hear the shrieking laughter of the Waspgnat. She tried to block it out of her mind.

When they reached the large metal doors, Olive gently set the exhausted Blanche on the ground and began to hammer on the door. Toots and Elizabeth joined her. But the doors didn't open. Perhaps all the fairies had already left.

The entrance to the landing bay was at a T-junction in the corridor which meant that besides the corridor they had just hurried down, there were two other corridors which led to the doors. Toots looked to the left and Olive to the right and both of them screamed as, with a loud and hideous clatter, the furzeweed broke into these corridors simultaneously. Now they were being attacked from all three directions at once. Their only hope was to get into the landing bay and then out of the Upside Down Garden.

Grey wraiths were swimming through the air towards them and the warm wind gathered strength. The corridor was dark with thorns. Olive hammered harder on the door, and cried out, 'Wing Commander Lewis, this is Olive Brown – can you hear me? Please let us in. This is an emergency!'

Suddenly Olive held up her hand. Elizabeth and Toots stopped pounding and Binky stopped barking. Olive pressed one ear against the door and stuck her finger in the other to block out the cackling wraiths. Toots looked behind and her heart leapt into her throat as the long wrinkled limbs and hideous head of the Waspgnat appeared at the far end of the corridor. It opened its horrible mouth and laughed. Smoke flooded out from between its teeth. Toots shut her eyes.

'Wing Commander, it's me, Olive Brown,' yelled

Olive.

The thorns were less than six metres away now and they were closing in quickly. The ceiling cracked and thorns shot down. The floor buckled and thorns shot up.

Suddenly there was a cry from the other side of the door. 'Brown, is that you?'

'Yes, Ma'am. Please hurry, let us in!'

Then above the noise of the furzeweed and the wraiths, Toots heard the bolts shooting back and the bars being lifted from the other side of the door. Suddenly the doors opened just wide enough for them all to slip through.

Olive made sure that Blanche, Palydia, Binky, Elizabeth and Toots were safely through, then quickly went in herself. Once inside they all leaned against the doors to try and close them before the furzeweed or the wraiths could force their way in. The Waspgnat scuttled forward and thin wisps of its horrible smoke streamed towards the open door.

Toots and Olive and all the fairies pushed harder, but just as the door closed the tiniest wisp of the Waspgnat's smoke blew into Toots's face and the Waspgnat's voice echoed in her head.

'Who do you think brought me to the garden? Who do you think?'

CHAPTER THIRTEEN

~ Landing Bay Number One ~

There was quite a crowd in the landing bay. Every fairy from the UDG was there and they all looked exhausted. Even so, several of them rushed to help Olive and Elizabeth carry the sisters into a quiet corner. Blanche and Palydia complained bitterly.

'No . . . ho. We don't want to sit down. We're not tired,' they wailed in their whiny child-like voices. But they were very tired, for the instant they lay down they fell fast asleep and started to turn into chrysalises.

Toots didn't help with settling the sisters. She didn't help the fairies bar the door. And she didn't notice that the fairies weren't leaving the landing bay as fast as they could. Toots just stood and stared at Wing Commander Lewis as the large fairy walked back to the table where the Group Captain was studying a map.

Toots felt a tap on her shoulder. She turned and found Elizabeth looking up at her.

'They're fast asleep now,' she said, nodding to where

Blanche and Palydia slept in the corner. 'They won't wake up until the summer and by then they'll be two of the finest, fattest bluebottles you'll ever see.'

Toots nodded, but she didn't have time to think about the maggots. She turned away from Elizabeth and stared again at the Wing Commander while the Waspgnat's voice screamed in her head.

'Who do you think brought me to the garden?' it cackled. 'You know, don't you?' Of course she knew.

Outside, the wraiths screeched and the furzeweed pounded against the doors, threatening to break in at any moment.

Toots's anger grew and gnawed at her insides as she watched the Wing Commander talking so earnestly with the Group Captain. She couldn't stand it, the Wing Commander was such a liar, such a hypocrite, pretending that she cared about the garden when Toots knew that she was just waiting for her chance to take over.

When the Wing Commander finished speaking the Group Captain looked up and summoned Olive to the table. Olive stood in front of the Group Captain with her head bowed. Toots couldn't see Olive's face and she couldn't hear what the Group Captain was saying, but she could guess what was happening. Olive was being told off for disobeying orders. Olive was being reprimanded for seeking out the Waspgnat. And all the time the Wing Commander stood behind the Group Captain, saying nothing in Olive's defence. Nobody noticed as Toots crept closer to the table.

'This is very serious,' the Group Captain was saying. 'I'm afraid, Olive, that you're going to have to take full responsibility.'

'Yes, Ma'am, I know. I'm sorry,' answered Olive hanging her head.

This was more than Toots could stand.

'Stop,' she screamed, rushing to the table. 'It was nothing to do with Olive. It's all the Wing Commander's fault.' Toots pointed at the Wing Commander. 'She did it! She brought the Waspgnat to the garden!'

Everyone in the landing bay became very still. Toots looked around. Olive, the Group Captain, the Wing Commander and all the fairies were staring at her. Beyond the doors, the furzeweed had stopped pounding, and the wraiths had ceased their screeching and the only sound that could be heard in the room was the soft giggle of the Waspgnat. It felt as though the whole world was waiting to hear what Toots had to say.

'It's all her fault,' Toots said again, but this time she didn't sound quite so sure of herself and her voice cracked a little. Toots looked from one puzzled face to the next. She had to make them understand. 'Don't you see?' she cried. 'The Wing Commander brought the

Waspgnat here. She did it so that she could take over the garden, so that she could get rid of the Group Captain. Don't you understand, the Wing Commander did it!'

The Wing Commander sighed deeply and the silent fairies sadly shook their heads.

'It is her fault,' said Toots weakly, but she knew that the fairies didn't believe her. Everything had seemed so clear to her a moment before, but now all her thoughts were fuzzy and muddled. One hot tear slid on to her cheek. She felt so foolish.

Toots could tell from the looks of amazement on the fairies' faces that she'd let her imagination get the better of her. Because she'd wanted to believe in the old stories, because she'd wanted to believe that the Wing Commander had brought the Waspgnat to the garden, she'd made herself believe it. But now she knew that Olive and the Group Captain had been right. The old stories were just old stories.

Suddenly the Waspgnat's soft giggle rose into a screaming laugh and the furzeweed began to pound and the wraiths to screech anew.

'Oh,' cried Toots, clamping her hands over her ears.

The Wing Commander shooed the other fairies back to their work and Olive gently wrapped an arm about Toots's shoulders and guided her to a chair.

'I've made such a mess of things,' sobbed Toots.

'It's all right,' replied Olive. 'You just got hold of the wrong end of the stick, that's all.'

'But I thought . . .' began Toots, 'I thought I knew better than you. I thought it was the Wing Commander's hate and anger that brought the Waspgnat to the garden. I thought she was jealous of the Group Captain, that she wanted to take her place.'

'Oh no,' said Olive softly. 'The Wing Commander is the Group Captain's best friend. She would never do anything to harm the garden. I told you, she's just gruff, that's all. Underneath, she has a heart of gold.'

'But I thought that she hated being told what to do by someone so much smaller and younger than she was.'

'Oh dear, you did get muddled, didn't you?' said Olive gently. 'Don't you remember I told you that the higher ranked a fairy gets, the smaller she grows? Sky fairies can hardly be seen at all. Everyone knows that our Group Captain is much smarter than all the rest of us put together and no one knows that better than the Wing Commander. You see,' she said patting Toots on the shoulder, 'the Wing Commander was once a Group Captain herself. She knows what it's like to lose a garden and she would never let that happen to her best friend. She was once in charge of a fine garden down by the river, but when the human in the garden fell out with his son it brought a Wasp . . .' Olive stopped herself. She had said too much. 'Well, come on, we've got plenty to do and that . . .'

Toots slowly lifted her head. 'But . . . wait . . . you told me there was no truth in the old stories. Even the Group Captain said that they were just old tales . . . ' Toots looked at Olive. 'If those old stories are true, why did you tell me they weren't?'

'Because we needed your help,' said the Group Captain, standing beside Toots. 'And we didn't want you to get upset.'

'What do you mean? Why would I get upset if you told me?' asked Toots. Then suddenly she knew. She closed her eyes and groaned. Everything seemed to come together at once. She remembered how the Wing Commander had said that 'humans usually cause all the trouble in the first place.' She remembered how Olive had said that the Wing Commander had lost her garden 'when the human began to fight with his son.' But, clearest of all, she remembered the day she'd first heard the Waspgnat's horrible laughter in the wind. It was the day she had fallen out with Jemma.

Once more the Waspgnat's question roared through her head. 'Who do you think brought me to the garden?'

'It was me, wasn't it?' she said quietly. 'I brought the Waspgnat here, didn't I?' Toots opened her eyes and looked around. All of the fairies had stopped what they were doing and were staring at her. Toots could see by their sympathetic looks that they all knew, that they'd always known. She felt wretched.

'Why didn't you tell me?' she cried.

'We couldn't. You had to work it out for yourself,' said the Group Captain softly. 'Olive thought that if you did you'd be able to help us beat the Waspgnat. That's why she brought you down here, but perhaps the Wing Commander was right all along, it was too great a risk.'

Toots looked over at the Wing Commander. Now she knew why the Wing Commander didn't like humans and she couldn't blame her. This would be the second garden she'd lost because of them, and Toots wished with all her heart that it wasn't so.

At that moment the Wing Commander looked at her, but Toots couldn't bear to meet her gaze so she turned away and buried her face in her hands.

Beyond the doors the wraiths squawked dementedly and the furzeweed banged so violently that the walls were beginning to buckle under the pressure.

'Come on, Toots,' said Olive as she gently took hold of Toots's wrist and tried to pull her to her feet. 'We have to find a way out of here and we need you to help us. Come on. You have to look at these maps.'

'Olive, I can't,' replied Toots who wanted just to sit in her seat and feel bad.

'You must,' insisted Olive pulling harder and forcing Toots to her feet. 'You can't dwell on the past, you have to deal with the present. Now look at this.' Olive made her stand beside the Wing Commander at the table.

It was only then that Toots noticed that there was something very wrong in the landing bay. With the threat of the furzeweed hammering at the doors the fairies should have been evacuating the landing bay as fast as they could and yet not one of them was leaving. Toots soon discovered the reason for this. In the far corner a group of fairies were digging holes in the floor, while others were chipping away at a mound of rock. Neither group was having much success. Toots stared at the rock. It almost covered the whole wall at the end of the runway and was completely blocking the fairies' exit.

'There's the problem, you see,' said the Wing Commander. 'That rock is fairly new. It wasn't there the last time we used this landing bay which was over a month ago.' She pointed to the map on the table. 'We think that our maps might be woefully out of date. We're trying to dig our way out through the ground, but we keep hitting stone. If only we had a more recent map.'

'This is absolutely the last available runway,' added the Group Captain over the furzeweed's terrible racket. 'It's our only hope of escape and if we don't find a way out soon, it could be . . . ', the Group Captain swallowed hard, but was unable to go on.

'Don't worry,' said the Wing Commander. 'Toots will find a way. I'm sure of it.'

This took Toots by surprise. She glanced up nervously and was amazed to see that the Wing Commander was looking at her with a strange glint in her eye.

Toots turned back to the table and stared at the map of the garden. It was highly detailed and showed all the tunnels beneath the ground and the locations of the landing bays, all but one of which had been crossed off with a large red X. Lying on top of this was a sheet of tracing paper which showed a plan of the garden as the humans knew it. This way, the map showed both the real garden and the Upside Down Garden at the same time.

Toots stared at it. There was the tree and the path and the fishpond and the beginning of the house, and there was the lawn and the flowerbeds, but something was missing. She shook her head. What was it? The garden in the drawing looked somehow out of date. That was it! This map must have been made before her father built the patio up by the house, before he put down the crazy paving!

Toots grabbed the Wing Commander's pencil. 'Look,' she cried. 'My father has just covered all of this area with paving stones, but they're not regular, they are strange shapes. We call it crazy paving.'

'Crazy paving?' whispered Olive, the Group Captain and the Wing Commander together.

'Yes,' replied Toots as she quickly drew the crazy paving in on the map. 'It reaches from the house to about here. That's why you can't dig through the ground.'

'Stop digging!' bellowed the Wing Commander. All the fairies stopped. 'So how can we get through this?'

Toots ran over to the mound of rock at the end of the runway. 'Is this where the exit used to be?' she asked. The Wing Commander and the Group Captain nodded. 'This isn't a rock,' Toots cried, pressing her hands against the rough surface. 'It's cement. My father must have blocked up the hole with it when he laid the paving stones.'

Toots stared at the cement. There was so much of it. At the rate they'd been going it would take the fairies from now until forever to chip through it all. They would have to find another way out of the landing bay. Toots narrowed her eyes, then nodded.

'Binky,' she cried. 'Come here, boy.' Binky ran quickly to her side. Toots picked up a small piece of cement and held it out. Binky sniffed it thoroughly.

'Go seek,' whispered Toots. 'Go seek out there.' She pointed to the middle of the floor where the fairies had been digging and, with one quick yap, Binky scampered over and set his nose to the ground.

Outside, the furzeweed banged harder against the doors, the wraiths screamed and the Waspgnat laughed. Inside, everyone watched to see what Binky would do.

Suddenly he stopped sniffing, then sniffed again, then stopped and wagged his tail. He began to scratch at the earth. 'There it is,' cried Toots. 'Dig where Binky is digging and you'll find the cracks between the paving stones. There'll be less cement there and it will be easier to break through.'

'Everybody dig where the dog says,' cried the Wing Commander. 'Good work Toots,' she said out of the side of her mouth. Olive nudged Toots with her elbow.

All the fairies quickly set to with their picks and hammers, chipping away along the line that Binky indicated. It didn't take long. Within minutes the cry went up. One fairy had chipped a tiny hole right through the cement and could see daylight beyond it. The fairies now worked together to make the hole bigger and it was only a matter of moments before it was just large enough for a fairy to squeeze through without crumpling her wings.

'Will everyone be able to get out of that hole?' asked Toots looking at the large Wing Commander doubtfully.

'Ssshhh,' whispered the Wing Commander. 'We don't want the Waspgnat to know our plans. Don't forget it can read our thoughts.'

Just then there was a loud scream from the fairies who were guarding the doors. One long sharp thorn of furzeweed had managed to squeeze between the crack in the doors and it was now forcing them open.

Toots, Olive, Elizabeth and the Wing Commander hurried to try and shut the doors. But the furzeweed was very strong and now that it had one thorn through, who knew how long it would be before the rest of it followed?

'If only I felt hungry,' gasped Elizabeth as she pressed hard against the door. 'It used to be my favourite food. I'd have been able to chomp through a thorn like this in no time at all. That's why the maggots muzzled me. They didn't want me to eat their beauty cream. Hah, they didn't know that I wasn't hungry. I haven't been hungry since I lost my little ones. I haven't been hungry at all.'

Toots jumped when she heard this and her eyes lit up. 'You mean,' she whispered, an idea forming in her head, 'you mean that you would eat this if you knew where your children were?'

'Faster than a fairy can fly.'

'Careful, Toots,' urged Olive. 'Please be careful. Remember that the Waspgnat is close enough to be able to read your thoughts.'

'And what about your children, do they like furzeweed too?' asked Toots, suddenly remembering the baby mites in the tree trunk. The hungry baby mites. 'Would they eat it if they were here?'

'Oh yes, they have fine appetites.'

'I . . . I . . . I . . . ' Toots could hardly speak because she was so excited. 'Olive, Elizabeth, I know where they are.'

Elizabeth's face lit up. 'You do?'

'They're hidden in a knot halfway up the tree, I saw them there this morning.'

'Were they all right?'

'They said they were hungry. Very hungry.' Toots's eyes twinkled.

The Wing Commander beamed at her. 'Can you hold this without me? I must tell the Group Captain,' she said.

Elizabeth nodded. 'I'll do better than that,' and she reached up and quickly took a huge bite out of the thorn and then another and another until it was almost gone. Another thorn shot through and Elizabeth bit into this one too.

Olive hurried to the Group Captain. Within moments the Wing Commander barked, 'All fairies are to fly immediately to the knot halfway up the tree, recover hidden treasure and bring it back here immediately, but none of you are to think about this mission. Remember that all your thoughts can be read. Be careful.'

Then one by one the fairies slipped through the hole and out into the garden. Olive returned to the doors and pushed against them.

Soon only Toots, Olive, Elizabeth, Binky, the Wing Commander and the Group Captain remained in the landing bay.

Although Elizabeth quickly ate every thorn that squeezed through the doors, she was starting to get full. The furzeweed was forcing the doors further open and everyone had to double their efforts to keep them closed.

'I wish they'd hurry back,' said Toots.

'Stop thinking about it,' warned Olive.

Toots nodded and tried to think of nothing. But her mind was racing, it was full of thoughts.

'I can't think of nothing,' she said. 'I keep thinking of things.'

'I know, it's hard,' puffed Olive. 'But if you can't think of nothing, think of something in the past that isn't important. Or say one phrase over and over again. That should still your thoughts.'

So Toots tried to think of what she could say over and over again that would make her thoughts stay still and not let the Waspgnat know what was going on in her head, but she couldn't think what to say. She tried a tongue twister, 'she sells sea shells on the sea shore. . .' but it was too hard and she soon gave up. She tried just to say butter over and over again, but her mind soon wandered. Then suddenly she hit upon something that Olive had said earlier. And as she repeated it, she felt her mind hold absolutely still. She had never felt so clear-headed before.

'We've got to get to the root of the problem. Get to the root of the problem. Get to the root of the problem,' she said. 'The root of the problem.'

The furzeweed pushed the doors open just a little wider and more thorns shot through. Elizabeth could only eat so much. Everyone pushed against the thorns, but they couldn't shut the doors.

Beyond the tangle Toots could see the Waspgnat with its horrible limbs crushed into what had been the fairies' corridor. Its disgusting face bulged as its mouth opened wide to laugh and there embedded in its chest was the Olm. Toots wished with all her heart that she could have broken that stone and robbed the Waspgnat of its power. But as she thought this the Waspgnat laughed louder and its wraiths darted towards her.

'The root of the problem, the root of the problem, the root of the problem,' Toots shouted in her mind to block out her thoughts. Then, suddenly, she had an idea and her eyes opened wide. It came to her in a flash and was so dangerous and so wonderful that she quickly hid it deep in her mind, so the Waspgnat wouldn't hear it. She knew she mustn't think of it. She knew she'd never be able to act on it if she did.

Instead she concentrated on pushing the doors shut. With one almighty shove Olive and Toots and Elizabeth managed to close the doors enough so that the Wing Commander could fix a wooden bar across them. That would hold them for a little while. Toots knew that she had very little time. She had to act fast.

'Olive, I have to go now,' she said, trying to fill her eyes full of meaning so Olive would understand that she wasn't just running out on her.

But Olive didn't understand. 'What?' she gasped.

'You have to send me back now. And Binky too.'

'But we need you here. That bar could break at any moment. You have to help us hold off the furzeweed till the others get back.' Olive's face was turning pink. 'You can't go now. You promised to help us!'

'I have to go. Please send me back now.'

Olive was furious. 'Why?'

'I can't tell you. If I could, I would, but I can't. I'll tell you later. I promise.'

The furzeweed banged against the door. The bar bent and strained.

'There may not be a later.'

'Olive!'

'I thought you were my friend, Toots. Friends aren't

162

supposed to let each other down, they're not supposed to keep secrets from each other and they're not supposed to break promises. Three simple rules, Toots.'

The words stung. 'Olive, please!' Toots begged.

'You'd better go if you're going,' said Olive coldly.

But the Wing Commander, who had been watching Toots intently, stepped forward. 'It's all right, Brown. I'll send her back,' she boomed. 'Come on then.' She took Toots by the shoulder and led her to the hole.

Toots scooped Binky up in her arms and looked back at Olive one last time. But Olive wouldn't look in her direction.

The Wing Commander knelt down beside Toots and fastened one end of a cobweb rope to Toots's ankle. She furtively pulled out a clean white handkerchief and tucked it in Toots's pocket, then she said in a quiet voice that only Toots could hear, 'Good luck, Toots, with whatever it is you're planning to do. This hankie will help you to remember us when you return to your world.' The Wing Commander looked into Toots's face and smiled. 'I think I'm learning new things about humans today. You've been so very brave already. There're not many of us who have faced a Waspgnat and survived to tell the tale.'

Toots's eyes grew wide. 'Then it was you,' she gasped. 'You were the fairy who knew about the Olm. You were the one who tried to save the other garden.'

'Shush,' said the Wing Commander as she finished tying the rope. 'Better if we just keep that our secret.' Toots suddenly saw the Wing Commander in a new light and she would have said something, but the Wing Commander stood up briskly.

'Off you go then.' she said in her normal rough voice. But Toots had to say one last thing. She leaned forward and whispered urgently, 'Please, you must make sure that all the fairies keep over to the far side of the landing bay. I don't want anyone to get . . . '

'Shush.' The Wing Commander put a warning finger to her lips and nodded. 'I'll make sure it's done. Hurry now. Goodbye, Toots, and be brave.'

'I'll try, I promise,' replied Toots.

Just before she left Toots tried once more to catch Olive's eye, but Olive still wouldn't look at her. 'She'll understand later,' thought Toots.

Toots nodded at the Wing Commander, then slipped through the hole towards the endless sky clutching Binky in her arms. As she hung by the slender thread of the cobweb rope, Toots stared up at the crazy paving above her and watched the huge yellow and grey stones grow smaller. Far away in the shadow of the tree the squadron fairies were setting off with their arms full of the hungry baby mites.

Toots didn't think of her idea, she knew better than to do that. Instead she kept it hidden like a secret deep inside her. She tried to keep her mind blank, but she couldn't forget the look on Olive's face as she'd left. Olive should have known that Toots wouldn't just leave her in the lurch. Toots wouldn't break a promise if she could help it. Why couldn't Olive have had a little faith? She was being unfair and it hurt.

Toots was so lost in these thoughts, that she didn't realize she was back to her normal size until she hit the ground with a bang. The paving stones were cold and hard beneath her knees. She felt the cobweb rope yank against her ankle, then slip away. The Wing Commander must have taken it back, she thought. Toots stared down at the little hole in the cement between the paving stones. It was a tiny crack, no bigger than an ant's hole.

'I won't let you down, Olive,' she whispered. 'I won't let you down.'

CHAPTER FOURTEEN

~ Back in the Garden ~

Toots knelt on the ground and ran her hand over the smooth paving stone. If she was correct, the Waspgnat was not too far from the second crazy-paving stone on the right of the hole. She put her ear to the ground and listened for the Waspgnat's evil laugh, then she picked up a pebble and used it to scratch a big X across the paving stone.

Toots leapt up and hurried to her father's tool shed. Binky ran after her, barking at her heels. She flung open the tool box and grabbed a chisel, a screwdriver and a hammer and she was about to run back into the garden when she noticed a long-handled sledge hammer with its blunt mallet head leaning by the door.

'That would do the trick,' she thought, 'if I can lift it.'

Toots put down the other tools and picked up the sledge hammer. It was extremely heavy, but with an effort she dragged it out onto the crazy paving.

Toots clapped her hands close to the hole in the paving stone.

'Everybody out of the way,' she warned any of the invisible fairies who might be flying by, carrying baby mites. 'Shoo. Stand back.'

She picked up the sledgehammer and, holding it with both hands, swung it up above her head, then let it drop with an almighty crash right on the X. A great crack ran across the paving stone from one side to the other and thin wisps of black and grey smoke trickled out. But the stone was not broken. Toots took another deep breath and lifted the hammer. She slammed it down again. The crack in the stone widened, but still it did not break.

'This time,' she said. She spat on her palms and rubbed her hands together, then lifted the hammer above her head once more. 'This time I'll get you.'

She smashed it down with all her might. The paving stone shattered and clouds of black smoke billowed out around the head of the hammer and dispersed in the wind.

'Toots, what on earth do you think you are doing?' cried her father as he rushed around the side of the house. She had forgotten that he had arranged to be home early. She had forgotten that he was going to help Mr Phelps cut down the tree.

'My crazy paving,' he cried as he pulled the sledgehammer out of her hands. 'You've ruined it. What on earth possessed you to do such a thing?'

'Afternoon, Mr Wheate,' said Mr Phelps tipping back his hat as he came into the garden. He nodded when he saw the ruined paving stone and the sledge-hammer in Toots's father's hands. 'Getting rid of the paving, are you? Can't say I blame you, I like a nice big lawn myself. Much better.' Mr Phelps winked at Toots.

'No, I'm not getting rid of it,' said her father in his most exasperated voice.

'Looks like that young fellow wants to get rid of it at any rate,' added Mr Phelps, nodding down at Binky who was digging furiously at the smashed stone.

'Oh!' cried Toots's father. He grabbed Binky by the collar and pulled him away.

Toots gasped. Between the fragments of the smashed stone she could see the ugly gnarled roots of the Waspgnat. The foul thing was old and yellow and in the sunlight its limbs glistened with a vile stinking slime. It was disgusting and Toots, her father and Mr Phelps shied away from its sulphurous smoke with their hands over their noses. The Waspgnat wriggled and writhed furiously as though it was in agony. It seemed to be trying to burrow back into the dark earth. Suddenly Binky lunged towards it, pulling Toots's father off his feet, and with a snap of his jaws, bit deep into one of the Waspgnat's limbs and began to pull.

Toots quickly latched onto Binky's collar and tried to help him pull it out, but the Waspgnat was too strong for them.

'Dad, help,' she panted.

Her father grabbed onto Binky's collar and though they pulled together they couldn't shift the Waspgnat.

'All right now, let's work this as a team,' said Mr Phelps as he also looped his fingers through Binky's collar. 'When I count to three, everybody pull as hard as you can. One . . . two . . . three!'

They all pulled together and suddenly the Waspgnat shot out of the hole and Mr Phelps, Binky, Toots and her father fell backwards onto the lawn.

When they sat up, the Waspgnat lay smouldering on the grass between them. Its horrible laugh was now a thin squeal. It sounded like air escaping from a punctured balloon.

'Would you look at that?' said Mr Phelps, taking off his hat and wafting away the smoke. The Waspgnat writhed in the sunlight, desperately trying to find a way to get back underground.

'What is it?' asked Toots's father.

Binky yelped and ran to his water bowl. He drank noisily, desperate to wash the vile taste from his mouth.

'Well I'll be jiggered, it could be the answer to your prayers,' said Mr Phelps mysteriously. 'We'll have to wait and see.' He looked up at the tree thoughtfully.

Toots crouched down to look at the Waspgnat. Even though she was so much bigger now, it still sent shivers of fear running up and down her spine. She could see the thin yellow slits of the Waspgnat's eyes and the wide slit of its ugly smoking mouth. And there was something so evil about its hideous high-pitched squeal that it terrified her even more than its laugh.

Using a long stick Toots's father poked at the writhing mass of slimy tangled roots. He drew back wincing as the Waspgnat's mouth opened even wider and clouds of black smoke billowed out between its sharp little yellow teeth, filling the air with noxious fumes. With an immense effort Toots's father flipped the Waspgnat onto its back and the piercing squeal grew louder.

Toots gasped. There was the Olm embedded in the Waspgnat's chest. It was the size of a walnut. Now was her chance to save Olive, to save the garden. She knew that she had to get it. She stared down at the vile, stinking, writhing, evil creature. She didn't want to go anywhere near it, let alone touch its revolting skin and pluck the Olm from its chest. Toots hesitated.

Suddenly the Waspgnat twisted its hideous face towards her. It knew that she couldn't do it. It could sense that she was afraid. Then it started to laugh. Toots soon saw why.

Bending its rootish limbs backwards, it suddenly

scuttled like a spider across the grass towards the hole in the paving stone. Toots couldn't let it get away. She dived towards it.

'Toots!' screamed her father. 'Don't you dare touch that thing!'

But it was too late. With one hand Toots pinned the Waspgnat to the ground while with the other she plucked the Olm from its chest.

When Toots held the heavy purple stone in her hand a horrible vengeful scream startled all the birds in the street and sent them screeching from the trees.

Toots's father grabbed her elbow and yanked her to her feet. His face was red and he was furious with her.

'Toots, don't you ever do that again. That thing might be poisonous.' And with that he kicked the Waspgnat out of the way, not caring that it skidded perilously close to the hole in the paving stone.

Toots gasped as the Waspgnat wriggled towards the hole. It moved more slowly, but it was still very much alive and it was trying to get back under the ground.

Toots knew what she had to do. The only way to save the garden, to save the fairies, to save Olive, was to break the Olm before the Waspgnat had a chance to grow another.

'Toots, get away' commanded her father. 'Go on, over by the house. And stay there!'

Toots ran to the side of the house and Binky

followed. She tried her best to crush the Olm with her hands, but it was like trying to crush a rock. She hit it against the wall as hard as she could, but it didn't even mark it, let alone make a crack or dent in it. She put it on the ground and smashed a brick down on top of it, but still nothing happened. It wasn't even scratched. Toots looked back at the Waspgnat. It was closer to the hole now. If it slipped into the ground, it might be able to grow a new Olm and then the garden would never survive.

Toots turned the Olm over in her hands. The purple stone was as smooth and as hard as a marble. What could she do to get it to break? What could she do?

'Hi, Toots,' said a small voice. Toots jumped and looked up. Jemma was standing at the garden gate. Toots didn't say anything, she just scowled and would have turned away, but at that moment the Olm began to vibrate in her hand.

Toots looked down at it, then back at Jemma. Jemma smiled a timid smile, then turned and set off down the street.

Suddenly Toots saw just how much she had hurt Jemma. She'd been hurt the same way when Olive hadn't understood why she had to leave when she did. It must have looked like she was running out on tthe fairies, breaking her promise for no good reason.

Suddenly she knew in her heart that Jemma hadn't

meant to let her down. She knew that Jemma must have had something very important to do when she hadn't helped her with the car wash, something that she hadn't been able to talk about at the time. Toots knew now how hard it was to let a friend down when you truly couldn't help it. And in that instant Toots understood what friendship really is. It isn't about doing favours and owing someone something or giving them presents, or anything like that. It's about trust and forgiveness and love.

'JEMMA!' Toots called as loud as she could. 'Jemma come back, please.'

The wind screamed through the garden.

'JEMMA!' Toots rushed down the path and flung the gate open wide.

'Jemma,' she called as loud as she could. 'Jemma, please come back!'

And as she did this the marble-hard stone in her hand crumbled like soft chalk. Toots opened her hand and a fine purple powder, which was all that was left of the Waspgnat's Olm, blew away like sand in a storm.

Toots grinned as Jemma hesitantly made her way back to the gate. She wanted to say something welcoming, something that would let Jemma know that she wanted to be friends again, but she didn't get the chance, because at that moment her father yelled excitedly from the back garden.

'Toots! Toots, quick! Come and look at this.'

Toots grabbed Jemma by the hand and pulled her through the gate. Together they rushed into the back garden.

'What is it, Dad?' panted Toots.

Her father raised his eyebrows when he saw Jemma with Toots and would probably have said something embarrassing if Toots had given him the chance.

'Dad, what is it?'

'What? Oh yes, look what's happening to this thing.' He pointed at the ground where the Waspgnat lay writhing horribly.

Toots watched in fascination as the Waspgnat's smoking black limbs twisted in agony, clawing desperately at the air, then entwined themselves tightly around the pulpy centre of its being. It was almost as if it were strangling itself. The root-like limbs looped in and over themselves and squeezed tighter and tighter and the vile mouth opened and closed wordlessly. The Waspgnat had lost its voice. Before long all that remained of the Waspgnat was a small, solid black nugget like a lump of coal, smouldering harmlessly on the ground.

'Well, what do you make of that?' asked Toots's father prodding the small nugget with a stick.

Mr Phelps crouched down and in his gloved hand picked up all that remained of the Waspgnat.

'My grandfather once told me of a root like this,' he said, examining it. 'He said it was a vile thing that could cripple a garden, keep it in winter for ever. He said that they grew on bad feeling in a garden, that they thrived on anger and hate. Some folks thought my grandfather was mad, they said he talked to the fairies – maybe he did. I reckoned when I saw this thing come smoking out of the ground, that that was what you had. If it hadn't been for your daughter, you would have lost this tree for sure.'

Toots felt her cheeks flush. If it hadn't have been for her, the garden would never have been in any danger in the first place.

'What do you mean, would have lost the tree?' asked Toots's father. 'What's happened? Is the tree all right now? I don't understand.'

Slowly Toots looked up and her eyes followed the branches of the horse chestnut tree where tiny green buds were appearing one by one by one.

'Dad,' she cried. 'Dad, Jemma, look at the tree. Look!'

Her father looked up, then stared goggle-eyed at the tree.

'Buds,' he finally spluttered.

'And there's another and another and another,' Toots shouted, grabbing Jemma's arm and running round the tree.

'And look,' laughed her father, pointing to a handful of green shoots that were poking up through the dark soil.

'And over here too,' added Jemma, pointing at the rose trees.

Binky barked.

'What's all the shouting about? What's happening?' asked Mrs Willets, wiping her hands on her apron as she came out of the house.

'We've had a miracle,' laughed Toots's father.

'Aye, a miracle,' agreed Mr Phelps. 'A small miracle.'

Toots knelt down and gently touched the tiny fresh green shoots with her fingertips. She felt in her pocket for the tiny speck of the Wing Commander's hankie and wondered if Olive and the fairies would be all right now – she felt sure they would be. Jemma sat down next to her and tugged at the grass.

'You know I wanted to come and help you that day, but I couldn't,' began Jemma. 'I had to . . .'

'That's okay,' said Toots. 'You don't have to explain. It's none of my business. If it was something important, then it was important. That's all. Come on.' Toots jumped to her feet. 'Let's play on the swing. Race you to it.'

Toots and Jemma played on the swing all that afternoon, taking it in turns to push or be pushed, laughing like a couple of monkeys. Toots couldn't remember the last time she'd had so much fun.

And while they played more buds appeared on the tree and fresh green shoots shot up through the soil. But Toots and Jemma were too busy having fun to notice what was happening in the garden. They were too busy to notice that spring was coming at last.

CHAPTER FIFTEEN

~ In the End ~

Toots wasn't really thinking about the Upside Down Garden when she went to bed that night. She had many other things to think about. Jemma had stayed to tea and they'd played until she'd had to leave. They'd arranged to meet early the next morning to go and play on the beach. Everything was going to be all right, thought Toots, as she drifted off to sleep, but even as she thought this she had a terrible nagging feeling that there was something she had forgotten to do and she didn't have any idea what it was.

Toots's dreams that night were full of muddled nightmares. Yellow and black eyes floated through her mind and sharp green thorns punctured her dreams. Suddenly she woke with a jolt.

'Olive,' she gasped. It was still dark outside but Toots was wide awake. She leapt up and knelt on the bed, then, resting the top of her head on the counterpane as if she was about to do a headstand, she gazed down at the ceiling and smiled when she saw Olive buzzing a few inches in front of her face, flapping her wings in great agitation.

'Thank goodness!' shouted Olive through a large megaphone. 'I've been shouting in your ear for ages. There's trouble about all the damage you caused with that sledgehammer. The Group Captain asked me to come and fetch you. You'd better come. Hurry.'

'I'll come,' Toots whispered.

'Hold on to the underside of your pillow,' shouted Olive.

Toots did as she was told and could soon feel herself shrinking. Before long she stood next to Olive on the pillow.

'Ready?' Olive asked.

'Olive, I didn't mean to leave you in the lurch before, you know. I didn't mean to break my promise, but I couldn't tell you why I had to go. I couldn't risk the Waspgnat knowing . . .'

'It's all right,' said Olive not smiling. 'But the Wing Commander is hopping mad about all the damage you caused. You'd better prepare yourself. Now jump.'

Toots took a deep breath and jumped off the pillow. Olive caught her round the middle, then carried her to the window which was open just wide enough for them to slip through.

The garden looked both eerie and beautiful in the

light of the full moon. The wind was sharp and fresh and cold. The furzeweed spore had almost gone from the garden now, there were only the faintest traces of it in the corners. It was piled up like old snow when the weather's changed, but Toots hardly noticed it.

Was the Wing Commander really angry with her? Maybe she'd just imagined that the Wing Commander had smiled at her and said nice things when they'd parted. Toots shivered a little and wished she'd put her dressing gown on over her pyjamas. What sort of punishment was the Wing Commander planning for her?

Olive didn't say a word as they flew up towards the broken paving stone. 'You gave us all quite a shock when you did this,' said Olive.

'I'm sorry,' winced Toots. 'I would have warned you but . . .'

'I know you would have if you could. But try explaining it to the Wing Commander. Hold on.' Olive flew up inside the broken stone.

Inside the fairies' Headquarters it was a terrible mess. The furzeweed had gone, but the walls were full of cracks and holes where the thorns had burst through. The corridor was full of fairies hammering and sawing and painting and wallpapering and trying to fix the damage. When they saw Toots the fairies put down their tools and stared at her. Silently they shuffled back and cleared a makeshift runway for Olive and Toots along the corridor.

'Do you remember how to land?' Olive asked. Toots nodded and started to run in the air. But her mind was so full of worry about facing the Wing Commander that she didn't even notice how smoothly she landed.

Olive landed right behind her, then led her through the silent crowd of fairies and down the damaged corridor. The fairies fell in behind them and followed in a big group.

'What happened to the furzeweed?' whispered Toots.

'The baby mites ate it all,' answered Olive. Toots had the feeling that she would have said more, but just then they arrived at the assembly hall and Olive ushered Toots inside. The entire squadron of fairies followed.

Toots blinked as she entered the bright hall. The Wing Commander and the Group Captain were waiting for her on the platform and between them sat another fairy whom Toots had never seen before. This fairy was even smaller than the Group Captain, but she was much older. She had grey hair, a wrinkled face and she looked extremely cross.

'That's the Air Commodore,' whispered Olive. 'She hardly ever visits the gardens unless there's been a disaster.'

Toots gulped as Olive pushed her towards the

platform. She climbed up unsteadily and stood next to the Wing Commander with her knees knocking together. The Wing Commander scowled down at her. Toots took the handkerchief from her pocket and held it out to the Wing Commander.

Toots tried to smile up at her. 'Would you mind if I kept it so that I can remember you all?' Toots whispered timidly.

But the Wing Commander only scowled more fiercely. 'Certainly not!' she hissed and with that she snatched the handkerchief and stuffed it in her pocket as though she didn't want anyone to notice what she'd done. Then she stared stiffly out at the hall and waited in silence while the whole squadron assembled.

When all the fairies were there, the Wing Commander coughed and stepped forward.

'Ehem,' she said with her mouth wrinkling as though she was trying to hide a smile. 'I would like to inform you officially that the furzeweed has been removed from the garden, that the Waspgnat's Olm has been destroyed and that the insects are returning as I speak. At this rate all will soon be as it should in the garden.'

The fairies in the hall cheered and clapped and screamed with glee.

The Group Captain rose from her seat and waited for the fairies to settle down.

'However, there is one matter . . .' she said sternly. The fairies fell silent and waited. '. . . a very serious matter, which we must address.'

The Group Captain stared at Toots, the Wing Commander glared, and the Air Commodore scowled. Toots's face burned.

'This is a very delicate matter,' said the Group Captain. 'Toots took it upon herself to smash the paving stone, uncover the Waspgnat and remove its Olm, thereby causing untold damage to the Upside Down Garden and at the same time ridding us of the Waspgnat.' The Group Captain looked very serious indeed. 'I'd like to call upon our esteemed Air Commodore to decide what ought to be done.'

The crotchety-faced old lady got to her feet and glowered up at Toots. Toots shivered and her eye begin to twitch.

The Air Commodore sniffed. 'I think,' she began slowly, 'I think the only thing to say in this situation is . . .' she paused and glared at Toots. Toots didn't flinch, but her other eye began to twitch. The Air Commodore sniffed again. 'I think the only thing to say . . . is . . . well done Toots! Very well done indeed!'

Toots blinked in surprise as the fairies clapped and cheered even louder than they had before. The Air Commodore shook Toots's hand.

'In all my time as a fairy commander I have never

known a Waspgnat be driven from a garden. Marvellous. Marvellous.'

The Group Captain shook her hand too. 'Thank you, Toots, you saved my garden. Thank you.'

Then the Wing Commander grabbed Toots's hand and shook it and shook it and wouldn't let go, not until the Air Commodore asked her to. Then the Wing Commander blushed with embarrassment.

The Air Commodore clicked her fingers, then waggled them at the Wing Commander. The Wing Commander saluted smartly and picked up a bucket from the back of the platform. With a smile and a little bow she handed it to the Group Captain who handed it with a smile and a bow to the Air Commodore.

The fairies fell silent once again and the Air Commodore turned to Toots.

'Normally, if a human visits the Upside Down World, they forget all about us almost as soon as they leave. We like it that way. But, in light of the wonderful service you've done us, we would like to give you something to remember us by. Whenever you hold this bucket in your hand, you'll remember the Upside Down World and all your adventures here.'

'Thank you,' stammered Toots taking the bucket. 'Thank you.' The fairies cheered again. Toots grinned at Olive and Olive grinned back.

'Tea's up,' cried a fairy at the back of the room, her

voice loud and clear above the din.

'Oh good, tea,' exclaimed the Air Commodore. 'All that pretending to be stern has made me ever so thirsty. Let's go and get it.' And with a little hop she jumped off the platform and hurried away to the tea table.

Toots sat down beside Olive on the edge of the platform and examined her bucket. She was very pleased with it.

'I'd better take you home, it'll be light soon,' said Olive.

'Can't I see Elizabeth?' asked Toots.

Olive shook her head. 'She wouldn't know you anymore, I'm afraid. She's back being a normal mite with her children.'

Toots sighed. She missed Elizabeth. She'd grown to like her odd little mitish face.

Olive smiled. 'That's how it should be, Toots. If the garden is to become healthy again, all the creatures in it have to return to their true selves. The Maggot sisters are on their way to becoming big, fat, bluebottle flies and Elizabeth is a real mite once more. That's how it has to be in the garden.'

'I suppose so,' said Toots.

'It's nearly morning, you'd better be getting back. Shall we go?' Olive put down her tea cup.

Toots stood up and all the fairies, who were crowded round the tea table, fell silent.

'Good luck,' called the Air Commodore.

'Thank you, Toots,' said the Group Captain.

'Goodbye, Toots,' beamed the Wing Commander.

'Goodbye,' cried all the fairies together and they waved as Toots left the hall.

Olive led Toots back along the corridor towards the smashed paving stone and they were about to take off when Toots heard a strange rustling through the rubble. Something was coming. Toots held her breath and waited and watched and slowly a face with two beady black eyes and a long brown nose covered in soft brown hairs appeared around the edge of the broken stone.

'Elizabeth,' cried Toots, but the mite didn't raise its head or take any notice of her at all, it just carried on its way. Behind it trailed a long line of tiny mites, each one looking far fatter and healthier than the last time Toots had seen them. Toots smiled.

'Goodbye, Elizabeth,' she said softly. 'Goodbye, mites.' But not one of them looked up at her.

'That's a sign that the garden is getting back to normal,' whispered Olive. 'Things are just as they should be. Come on, Toots.'

Toots nodded and followed Olive. When they reached the broken paving stone she set off at a run. Olive flew behind her and picked her up and together they flew through the hole and down into the brightening sky.

Before long Olive set Toots down on the underside of her pillow. 'Goodbye, Toots,' she said with a smile.

Toots held her new bucket between her hands.

'Goodbye, Olive, goodbye,' she whispered as she felt herself begin to grow.

Olive gave her one last smile then, flapping her wings, she leapt off the pillow and flew to the window.

'Don't forget,' she shouted back across the bedroom. 'Whenever you hold your bucket you'll remember the Upside Down World.'

'I won't forget,' whispered Toots and then Olive was gone. The bucket was growing smaller as Toots grew bigger and soon she could hold it like a cup in one hand. Then it was only as big as an egg cup and then as only as big as a thimble. Toots closed her hand around it so that she didn't drop it when her world turned the other way up. She could still feel it in the palm of her hand as it grew smaller and smaller.

When Toots's gravity had switched and she'd reached her full size, the bucket felt no bigger than a piece of grit caught against her skin. No wonder it had pinched so much when she'd worn it on her finger like a thimble.

She sat on the bed and carefully opened her hand. It looked empty, but Toots wasn't worried because she could still feel the bucket there against her palm. She twisted her head to one side and could just see a tiny silver speck glinting in the early morning sun.

Toots opened the little drawer in her bedside table and pulled out one of her most treasured possessions. Inside a tiny velvet box was an amethyst ring which had once belonged to her mother. Toots carefully put the bucket on the little cushion next to the ring, then ever so gently closed the box and slipped it back into the drawer. The bucket would be safe now, but as soon as she'd closed the drawer Toots's memories of the Upside Down World began to fade. And Toots didn't even realize.

With a yawn she looked at her clock. Soon it would be time to get up and she was going to the beach with Jemma in the morning. She didn't want to be late for that. Toots snuggled down under the covers and was soon fast asleep.

CHAPTER SIXTEEN

~ The Next Day ~

When she woke up the next morning Toots had forgotten almost everything about the Upside Down World.

Olive and the squadron and Elizabeth the mite were like foggy memories from some half-remembered story, as vague and as hard to hold as a dream dreamed a summer ago.

Toots dimly heard the doorbell ring downstairs and a moment later her father called, 'Toots? Sleepyhead? Jemma's here.'

'Coming,' cried Toots and without another look at the garden or another thought or care for fuzzy memories of dreams where everything was upside down, she leapt out of bed and into her clothes, and ran down the stairs three at a time to meet her friend.

Toots
and the upside down house

Up on the pipe Toots was still talking through her chattering teeth. '. . . A bear,' she said. 'A great big warm hug like a bear'. And then everything went black.

When Toots stands on her head and sees a little creature scurrying across the ceiling, her whole world is turned upside down . . . and so is her house!

Follow Toots' fantastical adventure as she meets fairy cadets, emerald sprites, slug-riding goblins and screaming mould . . .